Holy
Smoke

Holy
Smoke

a novel

Anna Campion & Jane Campion

tmb
talk
miramax
books

HYPERION
New York

Printed in the United States of America.

For information address
Hyperion,
77 West 66th Street,
New York, New York 10023-6298.

Library of Congress Cataloging-in-Publication Data
Campion, Anna
Holy smoke: a novel/Anna & Jane Campion.—1st ed.
        p.   cm.
ISBN 0-7868-6349-8
I. Campion, Jane. II. Title.
PR9639.3.C278H65   1999
823—dc21   98-40596
                            CIP
Paperback ISBN 0-7868-8563-7

First Paperback Edition

Original Hardcover Designed by Christine Weathersbee

3 5 7 9 10 8 6 4 2

We thank our editor Lesley Bryce for her focus, forbearance, and skill; David Hazlett for his steely faith; Viccy Harper and Elaine Steel's enabling support; Susan Dalsimer's calm. Our daughters Alice and Eve, friends, and family. Christine Woodruff, our researcher. John Cleary, our religious advisor. Chris Murphy's legal foray. And the many other people who generously let us share their experience. Also, a special heartfelt mention to our extended family in Jaipur, who adopted us as their own.

Ignorance

Strange to know nothing, never to be sure
Of what is true or right or real,
But forced to qualify, *or so I feel,*
Or *Well it does seem so:*
Someone must know.

Strange to be ignorant of the way things work:
Their skill at finding what they need,
Their sense of shape, and punctual spread of seed,
And willingness to change;
Yes, it is strange.

Even to wear such knowledge — for our flesh
Surrounds us with its own decisions —
And yet spend all our life on imprecisions,
That when we start to die
Have no idea why.

Philip Larkin, 1964

Holy
Smoke

Pulse

HUMAN RESOURCE & DEVELOPMENT CENTRE

TO: Mr. P. J. Waters
FROM: Stan Mikle
DATE: 26 November 1998

Dear PJ

I'm hoping this fax finds you. It's over two years since we last spoke, re the Nelson boy, Greg, who by the way is apparently going wellish, if jobs, girlfriends, trendy gear can be a measure of anything. I'm still your desk-fat slob but enjoying every last inert calorie.

So I await a confirmation of your fax number as the material I have to send is highly sensitive. My regards to the gracious Carol, who I will never forget for all her support.

Yours,

Stan Mikle
Psychotherapist and Counsellor
P. O. Box 25, Prymont, NSW, 4210, AUSTRALIA
FAX 00612 91086610

P. J. Waters
Exit Counsellor
Apt. 7a
1193 Mitchell Ave.,
New York (212) 319-2349
http: / / www.vmail.net / Waters /
26 / 11 / 98 5: 52 pm

Stan,
Honey, thanks for your remembering of me. Yep
this is us, Mr. P.J. Waters and myself. Fax away.

Carol.

Pulse

HUMAN RESOURCE & DEVELOPMENT CENTRE

Friday, 27 November 1998

Dear Carol and PJ,

I am certainly grateful to find you at home. I have a case you might be able to help us with and it goes without saying if *you* can't help no one can.

We have a girl, Ruth Baron, a twenty-year-old Australian. Apparently she was travelling through India, usual old historic hippy trail, and she comes up against our old fiend Chidaatma Baba, now you see him—now you don't. Currently re-constructing out of Rishikesh. She's simply curious, but while sniffing about and giggling at the converts, she is personally targeted by old Daddy, he does the finger on the forehead shakti and the next day she's in sari, mollah, and digi the lot, burning her return ticket and preparing to take orders. Swears she's found the point, the truth and she's radiant. Well, this is all reported by her little accountant girlfriend, Prue Lemon, who scurried back to Sydney armed with photographic evidence.

Optimum freak out with the parents, father failing to recognise daughter in "national costume."

Mother more concerned with big smile. Not previously known as "Smiler."

We are worried about her here. She's a bright attractive girl, exceptional scholar, who apparently dumped it all at University level to make some $'s and do a bit of travelling.

Her parents want to bring her back and have her exited. She hasn't responded to their initial line of attack: "Please come home for Christmas—sending ticket to the Qantas office." So they have had to resort to stronger tactics: arrive in India and talk her into coming home. They have safe relatives on a farm in the country, country where the Dad's going to be "coronary," ill, and waiting to say his last goodbyes. It should be an ideal place for the exiting. The pace is on because the initiation day in India is two weeks away. We want her out before that.

The mother is apparently closest to the girl, so she has volunteered to fetch and carry, no small offer, you know India in December—party, party, party. The two older brothers are in on it and will be available to help, stressed need for secrecy. Plus we'll get some security support and Colin Weathers, who you liked, your assistant with the Nelson boy, is available should you want him. Anything else you need don't hesitate to inform. Please send an update of your fees and also your preferred travel arrangements, or would you like to handle that your end?

First things first, can you help?

Yours

Stan, on behalf of the Baron family
P. O. Box 25, Prymont, NSW, 4210, AUSTRALIA
FAX 00612 91086610

29/11/98

Dear Stan,

Yes thanks, my fees are still $10,000 plus costs. Carol will attend to all the travel details. Please inform when the girl is en-route to Sydney and I'll stand by to depart. Please explain to the family the utmost delicacy and seriousness of what I am attempting to do with their daughter. There must be no interference whatsoever once the three day process begins. They may be called in at any stage after day one to support or watch videos with us. Colin will be good as backup, so tell him now as you know I can't go in alone, ask him how's the word, is it still with God?

So Amen to you Stan and let's hope Mrs. Baron can get Ruth on that plane. The first step is always the hardest.

Keep us informed. We have a Moonie in Kentucky to show the sun on the 16th, after that we'll be back in NY.

Om Om Om and peace be with you brother
                                                    P.J.

p.s. I'll book on every airline leaving for LA after my three days. I don't fancy Xmas in an Ozzie jail mate!

Pulse

HUMAN RESOURCE & DEVELOPMENT CENTRE

Friday, 11 December 1998

Dear PJ,

Mrs. Baron departed day before yesterday, currently meeting Ruth in Delhi. p. p. s. on the subject of jails. Had an unfortunate powwow with Mr. Baron—the selective listener. Who'd conveniently woken up several hours after my kidnapping/ illegality lecture, had to rewind the tape while he paced round with his bum in a sling . . . ever counting the cost, tic, tic, tic.

Stand By—Stan

Pulse

HUMAN RESOURCE & DEVELOPMENT CENTRE

Saturday, 12 December 1998

Dear PJ,

Not looking good, Ruth is refusing to return, under their thumbs, she's "sorry" about her father "but maybe next time" (assuming he'll be back)—man! She doesn't want to miss the initiation.

Stan.

Pulse

HUMAN RESOURCE & DEVELOPMENT CENTRE

Tuesday, 15

PJ,

WE HAVE HER!! She's arriving in on flight QF 9 from Bombay in 14 hours. Mrs. Baron on emergency O_2 after asthma attack, the bloody Embassy saved our arse by insisting Miss Baron accompany her on threat of passport cancellation.

Stan.

1

My name is Ruth, "Ruthless" some have said like I'm some freak survivor and I admit my instincts are sharpened that way. Darwinian. Even when the family ganged up against me, more or less ordering me to undergo the three day ordeal I thought, Okay I'll do it, I'll wall off, meditate and survive him . . . He's just a fucking thug from New York. Give nothing, be nothing, rise above it. But I wasn't feeling steady within myself and my hand shook. The tremor started as I was running this "Handle it, handle it" dialogue—that's when I asked him (the deprogrammer) if I could talk to my mother and oldest brother, Tim.

He said, "Sure."

He said it twice, which calmed me right down, the sense that he was nervous too. I'm bad like that, I can feel other people's anxiety taking shape, looming above them, gathering in damp sweaty clouds across the room. I used to stand in front of my brothers counting, 1, 2, 3, 4, in a whisper. It drove them crazy . . . 5, 6, 7, 8 . . . It's not working on him though, I don't think he can hear me. His upper lip sweats, he looks directly at me. His eyes are smiley, wrinkly, really I'd say he's about fifty-four, fifty-six.

So we're standing on this grassy mound. I wish I could say it had distinction, but it doesn't. The grass is dry, the farmhouse is behind me, and behind the house are the hills. Space, miles of it without people, or it would be if we weren't all standing in our semicircle, all ten of us, staring at the red dust—them with their arms linked to keep me in. Mum comes over and stammers, "Puss's room," in my ear. I automatically click on my aunt who stands next to my uncle and sort of winks. I'm thinking, they're all winking and nodding but they can't be, why is Puss winking? She winks again. Puss is my mother's sister, she's married to Bill Bill, who's small faced, thin and giggly. They don't have children, they have emus instead, Puss calls them her "girls," high protein, low cholesterol meat packs, evil to everyone but Puss. Before birds it was cats, none of them liked anyone else either.

I trudge to the farmhouse, there's nothing else to do. I don't want to justify their madcap kidnap plan with lunatic scenes, pin downs, or mouth-frothing. I know what this is anyway, it's Prue fucking Lemon blahing on about spaced out sannyasins and Guru marriage.

Prue was my friend, incredibly past subjective conditional or what ever they call it. We'd both travelled to India in April, we didn't really know why we were going, we could have gone many places. Anywhere that wasn't known. Our knowledge was zero—pathetic as you'd expect. Taj Mahal, saris, elephants, bedspreads, and whispered gossip about Goa's party scene with dope, lots of lovely E, and no one persecuting you. Indians don't get on your case, they don't judge you, they judge themselves, self-deprecating like Woody Allen. I'm trying to remember a typical example. Well, typically they exaggerate praise:

"Oh you're so wonderful, intuitive, beautiful, fantastic, intelligent, tremendous . . ."—exorbitant blah. I asked this bloke Svi why he did it, why he exaggerated, he said, well he laughed, he said, "Gracious Roouth, who needs the truth?"

What I wasn't prepared for, though, what nobody told me about, was the rubble; one rubble town forming another rubble town, selling rubble to the rubble town. The buildings that weren't rubble had masonry missing, large chunks crumbling into established piles with over-sized gaudily coloured Krishnas or Shivas poking through. It all made sense as much as *Alice in Wonderland* makes sense, a biblical-stroke-diesel heaven and hell. I never knew which we were running into. We'd been warned of rape, we'd heard stories and stuck together after ten, stuck together period. The whole thing was like standing on my head and watching my brains run out through an hourglass. I'd see girls begging whose dresses were so caked in dirt they stood away from their bodies. I saw a beautiful white horse with thirteen men in exotic cos-tume stroking her. I saw a rickshaw with its front glass shattered having banged into an ox. I saw women with strangely carved prosthetic limbs. I saw sadhus with six foot moustaches. I saw exquisite dancers with snakes, child dancers with large kohl eyes. Sometimes I would see all of these things within minutes, sometimes in different mixtures somewhere else. People cleaning their teeth with sticks, men with bones sticking out of their legs, animal, human, animal, human, human, never a day I could predict.

In Sydney you know what you will see more or less without exception before you see it. Everything's regulated; you can't regulate India, no system could contain her and if you found one you'd only wreck the place.

After Goa we went on to Kulu and split up at the ashram out of Rishikesh. Prue wasn't happy with the atmos, washing facilities, or chanting. I loved it, it's complicated, but she wanted to go. I kept trying to describe how I felt to her, how my insides were going soft and warm, as if my hard chest plate had been ripped off and exposed to this warm human hand stroking up and down inside my innards. It was such a blissful state.

I couldn't understand her resistance. She wanted me to go back with her, she wouldn't hear my "No" so I burnt my airline ticket in front of her, then she believed me. She was sobbing, but people don't own you, they really don't, this is what gets me.

The bedroom was so darkened against heat, it was hard to see anything. My eyes adjusted to white raised daffodils on a purple background. Puss has always tried to make a nest egg effort, which is almost impossible on a farm. There was a pink sheepskin cushion on the bed I thought at first was a cat—wow pink! I plucked at the wool muttering internal mantras: "I won't be incarcerated, I won't be incarcerated." I lay looking at all the knickknacks, china cats, brasses, and wedding photographs. Puss's hair was set in a flicked-up bob, she looked fresh. Mum was always femme, buns and plunging necklines, eyelash tongs with curly startled eyeliner.

Puss is wiry with sensible undyed hair, colourful clothes, mostly purple, her favourite, and terrible Gaia tack earrings. There were cats on top of the wardrobes and book shelves. Stuffed cats, china cats, some linked to each other with brass chains, mother and three kittens. There were pictures too, hand painted efforts of kittens with popped surprised eyes and bulging cheeks—they looked as though someone had stuck a finger up their bum. God it was oppressive . . . I had morbid thoughts of them all sitting there trying to look cute, so when she dies someone else will come and take care of them.

I stood up, I wasn't feeling well, light in the head, cold chills down my back. I went and was sick in Puss's mauve rubbish bin, hands quivering, hardly able to hold the bin. It didn't smell much so I hid it in the wardrobe. Mum came in as I was cleaning my teeth, she was holding a bottle of mineral water, she sort of slunk along the edge of the bed twisting the top. Tim came in stretching a cup of tea towards me; I didn't take it, I let it hang there and spoke to Mum.

"Mum, he's a thug."

"Ruth, you don't know him."

"I don't need to . . . look at me, Mum, I've got joy in my life now. I'm really happy."

My eyes stretched in truthful appeal—"You always said you didn't care what we did as long as we were happy."

No one was happy.

Mum tugged at a tissue, Tim hung against the wall, he is handsome in a soapy kind of way, veins throbbing on the temples. I had to act, "do," Baba always said, "do, don't miss the opportunity." Persuade them I'm grasping at full consciousness, that every moment spent here is denying me further progress. Oh, fuck it. It's all so bloody, pissy, impossible with them—wedded to their mall instinct, crumbs of materialism.

"Okay if it's the marriage that's done this, I won't marry him, it's off, I don't need to do it, it was an honour, an honorary gesture. Baba's love for me, that's all, it was his expression."

Mum picked her lips. "I don't trust this, Tim, I find her too difficult . . ."

"What's difficult?"

"You, you've always been difficult, you used to say you were going to school, only you went to the library. Now I don't know where you are, I fear you've been manipulated, even drugged by these people."

"Christ!"

"Well I'm sorry but that's what I think. I believe you're manipulating me now." Deep nod to the mineral bottle. "We've come here to save you, Ruth."

"Well don't, save yourselves. For god's sake, Mum, why do you think we're here?"

"Where?"

"On the earth, tell me why are you here? What's the point of your life?"

Mum was listening, her eyes swivelling towards Timmy, "Is this a trick, Tim? You see she always does this."

"It's a question of meaning, Mum, what do you think the point of your life is? Do you ever think about it?"

Timmy stretched out the tea again, I took it, Mum scrunched tissues.

"Well aren't you interested in your inner essence different from every other essence? Aren't you curious about that potential . . . what it means to have created an individual you. I mean why? Why, should God bother? When most people like you treat it like accidental occurrence . . . I suppose that's the disappointment God prepares for—human complacency. But if it were possible to know, to really know why you were here, wouldn't you like to, Mum?"

The tissues mutilated.

"We haven't got time for this, Tim, he's out there waiting."

Tim pushed himself off the wall, mobile phone flopping onto carpet. He bent down after it. He was disgruntled, I could tell, he hates the country, stuck in a room dedicated to heterosexual bliss.

"Well, Tim?" said Mum, "I want you to say something, you can risk an opinion, can't you?"

"Well, I was thinking mistake, mistake . . ."

"About what?" I said.

"About you. . . ." he said.

"Oh fuck you, Tim!"

"Hold on, hold on, let me finish. I was thinking mistake, mistake, but now I'm inclined to a different opinion."

"Why?"

He folded his arms and stared at me. "Because . . . because your eyes look odd."

I laughed, crossing my eyes and batting the lids.

"Look," he said.

I looked.

"Mum and Dad have spent a small fortune on this guy, who by the way has a good reputation."

"According to who?"

"According to cult experts."

So I said, "So you think it's a cult do you?"

He said he wasn't qualified to say, and changed tack, going on hell for leather about the three days treatment and what it could do for me.

"Why not do the three days, it's only three days. What the fuck can three days do to you?"

I told Tim he didn't understand, that these guys'd deprogram anything: communists, lesbians, Jews marrying Christians, blacks marrying Asians. They do rough things.

"Jesus Tim . . ."

"Jesus what? You don't have to look at me like I bloody well killed you."

"Well, why are you siding with them then?"

Knock, knock, from the outside . . .

"Shit."

We all looked as the door opened. He was standing there, saying, "May I?"

Our mouths were slack, Mum vigorously nodding her head, phew written across it. And I looked at him, fully stared. Everything was pressed, his jeans, his collared T, jacket, hair. God, I felt depressed, an old time jock my father's age exploring my mind. He shook my hand, which I didn't want to do, he even enclosed it in his other paw, "Hi Ruth, pleased to meet you." Face smiling, confident, beaming in at me. He had wide cheekbones, nothing too big. His lips had a pronounced *V*, they were moving. "Could you," mumble, mumble (must have been go, because next my mother and brother leave the room). I don't protest, I watch, he's quieter than they are. He checks the door, turns into the room, pauses, walks towards me in a rhythmic slouch and talks sort of lullaby American.

"Ruth, I suppose you hate me already, not an unusual reaction given the circumstances. . . ."

My arms do an involuntary shiver. Of course I did hate him but pathetically I didn't want him to hate me.

"Call me John," he was saying. "Or PJ"—PJ Waters was his full name.

"Do you need a drink?"

I did, but I said, "No."

He said, "Good."

Then he went into this thing about us having to sort something out, on account of the fact my family had hired him and that even if I returned to India it would be in my best interest to hear him out.

I didn't speak, my mind filled with whys and receding hairlines. I was about to engage, when a face appeared at the window with a little wave. PJ noticed and went straight up and closed it. Robbie, my second oldest—"rock on youse chickie babes"—brother, looked all sheepish. His tongue grossly distended, stretched out and dribbling. Hand on pretended rope, in an (opps, opps) mock execution pose.

The family was driving me nuts, all this tiptoeing about, buddy buddy stuff. We all love you, and to prove how much we've hired our own special gorilla from AMERICA. The gorilla sits down near me, his face all sincere. "I can't concentrate round these shenanigans." His arms flap in exasperation. "Your family is too disruptive, we can't work here."

My face mirrors his in a series of blank and earnest gestures. I really want to laugh, the family put in such a fashion. I sort of nod my head conspiratorially, feeling sly. He continues: "The three days is an in-depth conversation we're going to try and have here. . . ." He presses the podgy bits on his palms.

"To open yourself to another person, to talk openly is a profoundly difficult business. It's not normally required of us. Our natural reaction is to defend rather than to explore our beliefs."

Yeah, and I'm thinking, I wonder why given our destructive capabilities. And he's going on about games and how we play them with ourselves and with others till that's all we do. My head's ballooning out all these sarcastic bubbles, like "Bend over now," and "Do you require lubricant?" He knew I was lolling about not focusing, so he stopped, looked really worried, pulled himself to attention, and began again in a concerned tone.

"The dialogue between the inner and outer selves is in constant dualism, in that sense we are always chatting away with an internalised other. Essentially dramatic. The strain for us as humans is not so much this internal dialogue, but the communication with the other that is not us."

My stomach churned, I felt stupid that it had, that I'd had some physical reaction. He stared round at me, fingers pulling at his collar.

"I guess you've thought about the damage that could be done to your core self, to the very centre of yourself if you were to, say, hand that centre over to someone else . . . the wrong someone else?" He leans forward, fiddling in his pockets, pulling out a box of matches.

"'*I feel within me that spark, that atom emanation of the divine spirit.*' Giuseppe Verdi. The soul is the match, the spark, the flame that can light your path."

He strikes a match, holding it out in front of him, his wrist flicking it through the air. We both watch the flame dwindle. He gets up and walks about, head tilted slightly, talking to the ceiling. I look up too, imagining it thick with flies, there weren't many.

"If I could arrange somewhere more peaceful for us to be, would you commit?"

Blah, blah, somehow I'd joined his words up there on the ceiling as he spoke them—so I said, "Yes," partly because I could see we would all be going on forever if I didn't and partly because I was nervous. Nervous about the idea of "No." "No" meant I'd have to justify with an energy I didn't possess. "No" means you really do care and I didn't care for him and his opinions. I lie down when I say yes, it usually means no, snore zzz . . . that my position was intolerable, and totally unconscionable still stood. However the family was worse; immolation I think you call it, when you offer up your prized sacrificial pig. They were victorious immolators.

Then he made his first mistake.

2

Yes, I annoyed her. I tried to hold the door open for her, she wanted to go to the bathroom, big deal—I didn't see the insult. Of course I knew she could open the damn door herself, but I like to see a woman looked after and again of course I know Ruth is a modern young woman, girl really, so she loathed my attempt at courtly behaviour. Which, perversely, I enjoyed.

Ruth as a case was simple enough. I *know* more. Religious ideas of whatever pomposity are obscure, with extensive research the client can't keep up. They crumble, as I knew she would. Ruth as a woman was completely different, and I pause here because there's some way in which she entered me and I'm not sure how. Not the devouring talons type, nothing so coarse, it was a kind of energy that needed to take something back. The overall impression was that I owed her, I *should* help. That's what it was, there was an intensity, I felt as if a fish had entered me and I couldn't quite decide if it was hot or cold. Usually when people sulk there's a dead energy. With her it was active.

Attraction is a complex, I noted it. Part of the reason for our paired approach, this business of our working closely with one another, partly so we can monitor the transference, counter-transference situation. Plus, maintaining reality checks and breathing space. It's our job to track the individual's progress out from Guru worship back to self. A methodical process. Often ex–cult members join us in the last throes, experienced back-up. And I don't mean the posse of mental illness that met me at Sydney airport.

I left New York on the sixteenth, dropped a day, arriving in on the eighteenth. I slept on the plane and was feeling stiff but in reasonable health. Landing time: 3:25 p.m.

First out to greet me was the sister-in-law, Yvonne, whose physical attributes were fairly obvious. Most notably her perfectly manicured lovely little hands. Pale freckles, big blue eyes. She was all over pretty, nice figure, very. She wore a pastel outfit, makeup, lots of hair clipped and constantly adjusted, the full feminine bit. Twenty-six, mother of one, married to Robert Baron. Prone to excessive talking, incredibly so, comes out in a rush:

"My name is Yvonne, you've probably heard about me." (I hadn't). "So pleased to meet you, so pleased to meet you, someone of your standing."—blink, blink— "Such a relief. Ohh, we've all been so tense wondering when you'd come. I'm on supplies, so if you need any of those little extras . . ."

Blinks, takes over trolley. New conversation:

"Do you find it hard to find polite help in America, people with lovely manners?"

I failed to make the connection here, did she mean she had lovely manners? People in America had no manners? It was peculiar. She was trying so hard I felt sympathetic; hovering there all twisted and pink. So I said, "I don't believe I've tried that yet." Actually my help wasn't particularly polite and I didn't want to think about it, it wasn't interesting to me to be thinking about it or to be going down this ridiculously obscure polite route anyway and yet here I was.

Two flicks to the hair, eyes up on husband. "Oh don't look at Robbie, he doesn't have any manners, do you?"

Problem: Nerves aside she didn't seem to fully grasp the gravity of our situation, the necessity for precise detail, utter concentration—the involvement of ourselves in a criminal activity, for instance.

Next out was Fabio; I don't like ponytails. Twenty-something, friend of Robert, well-worked muscles, blond, brown, supposed to be helping with security. Not all there in the head department. Example: crashes into an airport signpost trying to retrieve a set of car keys thrown dumb, dumb high by Robert. I have no idea why.

Robert (variants: Rob, Robbie), husband of Yvonne, brother of Ruth. Robert is big, around two hundred pounds (some of it porky), twenty-eightish, round-faced, jokey, immature, sloppy turnout. Has distorted ideas about his role in our operation: to me, minor security; to him—King. I really don't know what he thinks; he keeps saying, "Yep, exactly, not a problem." Unreliable.

Finally, Stan Mikle, my fellow pro, and the only one I could hammer out the facts with. Forties, albino skin, neurotic attitude to sun. Fatter than when we last met: roly-poly. Tried to steer the disorganisation, which got pretty silly with Yvonne preparing to sit on my lap. They'd miscalculated, we were too many, so I said, "Look, I'll get a taxi."

"Ohh noo," said Yvonne. "You get out, Fabio, you get the taxi!"

Stan anxious, mopping forehead, said he'd take the broken-nosed Fabio to a hospital and meet us later at the motel.

"Which one was it?"

"Yeah, where is it?" said Robbie.

No one knew. Yvonne hadn't booked it because there was just so much wonderful choice and she'd wanted me, Mr. Waters, to come visit them all.

That's when I should have left, when they were all arguing over my luggage, repacking the car. Chimps party equals *get back on the plane*. Instead I'm standing amidst the family in a very large, balmy parking lot. And I don't know whether it's the heat, fatigue, or what but their disorganisation has an odd intoxication to it, like flying into thick clouds—it's everything I fight against and now I wonder, Why? Just a glancing thought, like there's a charm to chaos. Being tossed about by waves so you don't know what's up and what's down. But finally you pop up and there's the sky, all properly and peacefully in it's place. For me it's a physical sensation of wooziness, a little sexy even.

Christ. I stop myself, thinking I must be some kind of pervert, and focus in on Stan.

"Stan, where is Colin, the guy with the exiting experience?"

Stan is looking shamefaced. I repeat the question. "Where is Colin?"

"He's had a family misfortune."

"Uh-huh." Now I can appreciate that no one can control, plan these events, or whatever, and he is trying to give me the details when a car trunk crashes down behind us. Yvonne has heard the words "lost" and "mother," a fatal combination. She's strutting over looking thunderstruck, her voice is shrill:

"Oh my God, no, Stan, don't tell me, oh no. What happened?"

"His mother died."

"Oh no, was it expected? Oh my God, Stan, what was it?"

I cut across her, "So he's not available?"

"Unfortunately not."

I pull him aside. "Stan ol' boy, we are in deep shit. This may be a maverick's game but I've got rules and I don't work, not ever, without experienced backup. Hypothetically, I would have thought that even on short notice, you could have gotten a considerable list of other candidates together."

"Mm, yes," says Stan and he's looking at me—stooping, in fact I see from his eyes that he's nervous, so I lighten up.

"It's a delicate us-against-them game, Stan. I'm already jet lagged and I need *her* tired, not me."

"Oh, I know, and I'm trying for a rabbi replacement, a very good bloke in Melbourne." He gives me his bottle of mineral water. I can see he's a big fan.

"Okay," I say, eyeing the bottle, repulsed by the amount of goop inside. "What's plan B?"

After a lengthy pause, I'm told the B plan is Fabio. "Couldn't he stand in for Colin."

I'm not sure if this is a statement or a question. "Stan, this girl—"

"Ruth."

"Yes, Ruth and I are taking a leap into the sky together. We're jumping out of a *fucking* plane. Now, before we hit the ground I need her chute to open, I need my chute to open. And basically, do I want to trust a guy who has just broken his nose running into a pole, with our parachutes? No."

Well yes, apparently, yes. Stan thinks Fabio's well turned out. He'd do a neat job.

I laugh at him. "Yeah, sure, Stan, sure, he'd do a neat job with his toilet bag."

And pace off under the trees, wondering about the waves and being tossed and whether we'll ever pop the right way up.

"It's dangerous. . . ."

"Hmm," Stan hangs his head.

He knows it's dangerous, he knows we don't have anything on Ruth short of declaring her mentally incompetent, which is extremely difficult to do. She'd have to have committed a crime, then we could scream "Patty Hearst"—overwhelming a vulnerable person's will. We could get some tame rat catchers, tame psychiatrists, to verify this. But we can't, she's not under eighteen, the international convention doesn't apply. Ours is a carousel of ends justifying means.

"Okay, okay, okay. What about your woman Carol then, couldn't she come out?"

Hell.

"I told you before, I could have gotten her out cheap on air miles, but now I don't know. It could take four or five days."

Stan pats me on the back. He's concerned for me. (Big deal!) He says he'll call the rabbi again. (Don't bother.) "Yep, he's top of the list, though there's others to try" (Do it.) 5:00 p.m. I was exhausted. The marooned expert, expected to self-duplicate and solve all the problems by myself.

Constant small talk—chat, amble, amble; I couldn't understand how they ever achieved anything. They kept it up all the way to the motel of choice. Everybody had a little conversation—the motel owner, more mouthing on about nothing, nothing that meant anything to me.

"Did ya hear what's required from the new cheerleaders in Queensland? Big brains and faces . . ."

Ha, ha, ha, HAH. Big laughs, I didn't think it was that funny. Then he says, "They're running it equal opportunities . . . ha, ha."

That's what's pernicious—there's no real reason for these conversations.

First night: We have a motel, I have a cappuccino, Yvonne swims and rises from the motel pool, all sane and pleasurable, till she stands dripping water on my foot. I'm astonished by the amount of water, perhaps it's a new swimwear material. She wants to know what I'm going to do with Ruth. My foot is soaked. I say:

"I'm going to talk in depth, I'm going to get down in the dirt with her."

Yvonne goes pink, she takes a gin and tonic from Robbie, who's busy arranging his alcoholic platoon beside a pile of peanuts on the mini-bar.

"A chance to experiment," he says, downing a Chivas.

Yvonne's talking. "You'd be very persuasive." She's talking to *me*. "I imagine you could persuade any woman to do anything."

Her eyes blink, a minor trance takes place.

I wade in:

"The thing is, Yvonne, I work on a team but I don't team date and I don't train to be persuasive romantically. I'm attacking the belief system, springing the trap, letting the mind loosen so it can think for itself. It's a dialogue. We float out suggestions, the clients sift those suggestions and choose for themselves."

"She's not that easy to chat to, is she Robbie?"

"Not unless she wants something."

"This isn't a chat, Yvonne, this is a conversation that takes three days to complete. It's a very intuitive thing. She's just come from an ashram where she's one of thousands. Here in this procedure she is unique. It's very flattering to have someone's undivided attention."

Robbie passes me a Coke. Yvonne sips her gin. "Well," she says, "I'd like someone to talk all about me for three days."

"Yeah," says Robbie, "someone other than you, you mean."

A pizza arrives. Fabio, nose swaddled in gauze, hands out the pieces.

Yvonne pokes me in the thigh.

"Yes, but what if it's love that you believe in?"

"Love's just as blind—I love you, I love you, I love you, and now I'm going to fuck somebody else."

"Ooh—I know, but what else is there?" Deep sigh. "Don't you believe just a tiny bit?"

"Which question shall I answer?"

Giggle, giggle. "Oh, hmmm, I don't know. . . . Yes I do, the second."

"Well then you've got the wrong guy."

She purses her mouth.

"Oh I don't think so."

I don't eyeball her, I should have. I want to get up, make some sort of bold move, but I wait too long. She moves instead. Sits directly opposite me, the soles of her feet touching, exhaling, her legs split apart. I look, internal voices tell me "Don't react." Her hands begin to explore the upper thighs, one leg is thrust into mid-air, her hands closely checking for nonexistent growth. My eyes drift down, into her close inspection.

"I got all this waxed for Robbie, so I can wear a string if he wants me to. Don't you think that's a little romantic? I love going to motels, everything's new, it's like having sex with a stranger. Just walking in, anything could happen."

Morning. Nineteenth of the twelfth, 6:00 a.m. We left the motel with its stucco units and miniature jungle, drove up Great Western Highway, Parramatta, Blaxland, don't know, don't know, they zipped past. Katoomba, I dozed off, saw urban sprawl, tarmac, huge trucks, muscly trees, and the same, same scenery for miles.

"What are they, those trees, what are they called?"

"Moreton Bays, Moreton Bay figs."

Beautiful bark, dark, thick limbs and huge smooth leaves I saw myself—tiny—sitting in one, propped up against the fork. Nice vision, probably brain affected by the heat and Robbie's dope waves. I thought I saw some marijuana growing beside the road, and said so, Fabio woke.

"Naw man, people grow it at home here, it grows like weed. I saw this house on the box, some westie was growing dope with his dad, they'd made a fence of it and the neighbours complained. It was on the news, aye. First the police couldn't be fucked so it grew to fifteen feet then some bastard video'd it; dwarfed the whole fucking house so the police had to come back and burn it down. People are pricks."

"Yeah but you have to live with them. . . . Heh, heh, heh."

Robbie's cigarette fumes waft in my face. Yvonne sprays some perfume on her feet. "Room freshener."

My head crashed, jerked up and over again, a black jet-lag sleep. I heard a child grizzle—Toddy, Yvonne and Robbie's boy. They'd picked him up miles back at her mother's place. "How old is he?"

"Four an' half. He still wears nappies."

"No he doesn't, only in cars."

"He does, he likes to pooh in them."

"Oh shush, you always exaggerate."

Toddy was piercing the top of an orange carton, orange spurting everywhere; I thought, I must tell Stan to get my lady, Carol. I must have someone to help me.

My eyes were struggling with a heavy pink bedspread, in the bare, forgotten room where Puss had hopes of a child, vaguely supplied by me on surrogate farm visits. Puss was my organising mentor. She and I liked lists and different coloured books with themes where we'd stick envelopes with yet more colour-coded systems for frequency of use, marked up *specials*, containing timetables. Mine were smudged with pawed-over finger marks, a result of excessive folding and repackaging. That's how I learnt to tell the time, scheduling imaginary bus and train routes for Puss.

In India I always woke with others, I hardly ever woke alone. (Indians don't understand Western obsessions with privacy, in fact I did wonder how they ever managed to masturbate but never asked.) Back here life's all functionality, what do you *do,* what job do you do? No tinkling of bells, chanting, or dancing, it's anti-pleasure, that's what's so sterile. It's not just the room, it's the never-ending cycle of practical joylessness. God! It's so bloody obvious, heart chakra . . . Fuck. Get up! Go teach Mum and Puss the fundamentals of meditation. We could go outside, and do it in the sun. The sun would help them detach and focus on the breath . . . the breath is really difficult to get, if I can teach them the sound, a sea over gravel sound . . . if I could explain it properly, that would introduce the taste!

That's how I was feeling on the morning of the nine-teenth, happy. I didn't suspect a thing, in fact I fell back to sleep meditating on the bed. Mum and Puss woke me up, peering in with their big eager smiles. I was so pleased to see them both smiling, I leapt out of bed and kissed them, put on my Indian flute ragas, danced round the room, got us all up twirling in mystical abandon. Heard Mum saying, "Look, look, it's the old her," and performed my whirling dervish, collapsing against the television. Mum was wheezing next to Puss, on the sofa, fiddling with her Ventolin.

I hop about and say: "I think I'll go and see Dad."

"Oh Ruth, I wouldn't disturb him right now."

"Noo, he's sleeping, he should be left alone." They look really anxious.

"Shit, he's not worse, is he?" I bound out the door, along the passageway, the two of them worrying along behind me. "He's really not very well . . . not very well." I tell them to stop it, I'm not even going to wake him. They slink back towards the kitchen, I go on, gently easing open his bedroom door. He's not in his bed. I hear voices from outside the window. "Dad?"

He doesn't reply, he's out on the lawn, head down in his pyjamas, whacking off a golf ball. The ball soars past the window, I rush outside, Bill Bill calls "Shot." Then sees me and freezes, appalled—his face pales, panic causing him to almost topple over. I look from one to the other.

"So you're not dying? Dad?"

He looks up, pretending involvement with his golf club. "No. Aren't you glad?"

"Of course I am . . . but you lied to me! You lied to me, Dad. Why?" There is no answer.

Dad takes a long sulky swing at another ball.

SHIT, fuck, I stamp around in shock. My body feels as though it's growing weights. I shut my eyes—this is not happening. . . . The stomping jars up through my legs, colored spots burst behind my eyes. They open to a far off hum.

Deliverance comes in a cloud of dust, fast-moving cars travelling towards the farm. Two cars, one of them Tim's, I can't quite see the other and am mad, angry mad. I've come all this way, for what?

My eyes snatch at Bill Bill juggling golf balls in mid-air, he misses them. *Plop.* I stare as they fall down in front of him, it's all so absurdly stupid I burst out laughing: *Plop.* He turns on me as if I'd somehow jinxed him.

"We're all sick from worrying about you, Ruthie."

"Why?" Button nose twitching, he reminds me of Tim Robbins.

"Yes, and there's someone here we want you to talk to."

"Who?"

"We want to be sure you're on the right track."

My jaws clench. "The right track?" God! I shouldn't speak, I shouldn't even credit them with this crap, but I do.

"Oh, so you'd know which track, would you? Well, thank you, Bill Bill, and fuck you all."

Their eyes narrow, little pig eyes of defiance.

"Ruth, it's a talk."

"It's fucked, Dad, it's really low. I'm taking your Toyota and I'm cashing it in."

They laugh at that. I laugh too, but I feel really anguished inside, as if I no longer know my own family, and am despised by them, an outcast. My eyes water with fear, I tell Dad I have to go, my whole body is saying: Go.

Go. I start to speed—what to do? What to do? I don't go anywhere, car doors slam in the distance. The car men and women are getting out—Yvonne, Toddy, Fabio, a stranger, followed on by Robbie. They're spreading out across the paddock moving towards us, smiling hard. The house is meters away, the keys to Dad's Toyota are sitting by his—ha!—hospital bed, they were definitely on the bed. Check the window, the window's still open. Do it.

I run. Dad chases me. I struggle up onto the ledge, one knee over, my arms pulling. I feel him clutching at my back. I kick, he grabs my leg and a fistful of sari, my body tips back on top of him. We're sprawling on our backs, leg-cycling insects.

He shouts, "Get that bloody sheet off, girlie."

We wrestle.

"How dare you!" I crawl away. He crawls behind me. God, we're like two sheep, I half expect him to mount me. Instead he unravels the sari.

"Fuck, stop it Dad, stop pawing me."

He's winding the material around his waist! I tug at him.

"You'll stay here and listen."

I lie on the ground snarling. Bill Bill taps Rambo on the shoulder, "Gilly, whoa there, whoa, let's wait for Mr. Waters."

Bill Bill lights a cigarette, Dad whisks it from him. "Just you wait, he'll sort you out girlie . . . You'll meet your match in him."

I pull the sari in towards me, Bill Bill helps retrieve the fabric, twists Dad's body round and round. Can't speak, I am so freaked out nervous, all my thoughts are on the sari.

The others walk up and surround me, "We love you, Ruthie. We're here because we love you."

Can't look at them, my throat makes strange, gurgly noises. I tuck and tuck, my fingers try to hold the pleats.

"We love you, Ruth."

God, fuck love. My stomach seizes up, I feel ill, it's hard like a cricket ball, a baseball, no an emu egg.

Yes and the way she did that tucking; concentrating, gathering herself to herself moved me. To be on exhibit and be able to transform that moment, a weak moment, where she's standing there as *freak*, into food for her own advantage was clever. Maybe innate, it was difficult to tell. As I debated, her head popped up and she looked straight at me—no ugly she and I don't mean solely in the looks department either. My eyes kept returning to her focused, tucking world.

She was winning. We were all at the heels of the struggling peach. That's what she looked like, all golden, not wanting our protection. I felt she'd had to struggle with a militant independence all her life and wondered what the downside of her position might be.

Probably the no man's an island thing, with us sea, she the island. Hard to stop significant others having expectations etc., whether she'd want them to or not isn't the point. They're going to have them anyway, they're going to go pluck their baby chick back from India if they feel threatened.

She was walking, zigzagging towards me, Robbie and Fabio on either side. When she stopped they stopped. Her eyes were on mine.

"I want to speak to my mother and Tim."

"Sure," I said, "sure," and didn't look away; I wanted her to and she did. I simply fixed on her and breathed. Her hair was short, not short, short, it sat off her shoulders, abstracted clumps—no not abstract, damn, I can't access the word, off-centred—oh, whatever. More importantly we had engaged. Openly I thought—just a look, a bounce back . . . something vulnerable she let me see. *Asymmetrical*—that's it. Yes. I knew then, I was the one. She did too, that's what had her so scared. My interpretation.

I confess when those three headed for the bedroom I had my ear to the door, she called me a thug. Based on nothing in particular, our first encounter, we'd barely spoken and now I'm demon seed, faith breaker of the faithful. A money hungry nut. Irrelevant. Horseshit: this wasn't about faith or money, it was a standard tantrum about me.

11:15. I pace and practice my speech: Stan, it's a gift, she's an open type of girl—we're halfway there already. . . . Yes, we made good contact. . . . Very. Well, I know it's not ideal, but then what is? You're an enlightened type of guy and I don't think we should be procrastinating. No, not in such precarious circumstances—could be dangerous.

I want to go it alone—that's the real message.

11:30. I call up Stan.

"Yes, yep . . . it was good contact. Uh-huh . . . very."

"Fabulous, you keep that going. And guess what, I've got Carol booked."

"Well, that's something, but I'll have to go in sooner."

"Why?"

"Because she'll take two days to get here, I haven't got two. . . ."

"John, you can wait till then."

"Yes okay, and we lose her. Very professional. I'm about ready now—and so is she. . . . No it's not all about me. We've got to think of stresses here. . . . You make the contact, and you go on in after. I need someone NOW. . . . That's right. I won't discuss the rabbi situation—someone who isn't materialising . . . Yes, it is how I feel."

"All right," he's hurt. I hear his voice crack.

"Sooo, what do you think we should do then—just let her go? Three little steps, Stan. It could all be over in twenty-four hours."

There's a very, very, long meaningful pause. Followed by a "Well you're the expert."

Ruth is in the toilet, without flushes or water. It's now 12:45 p.m., day one of our programme and we haven't gotten anywhere. One o' clock and she's still in the bathroom. There's an element of panic with this, I'm sure there's nothing going on, I haven't had a suicide but there's always the chance of a cutup you may not have preempted. At least if I've gone through the thought, I've somehow prepared and exempted myself—in theory: present to the idea of BASHING down the door.

Bill Bill's in the corridor, he puts his finger to his lips. He's got a cigarette he's not supposed to have, he delivers this part sign language by rolling up his T-shirt and showing me a dull pink nicotine patch. I take advantage of this intimacy to push for a quieter environment. He has a halfway hut, he tells me, "It's not luxurious, haf, haf." He's got this precious pup laugh.

"Can Ruth and I use it?"

"You can."

I ask about supplies. He says, "Yvonne'll do that." I say, "Yes?" (large question mark implied).

"Oh, yes!" he says. "She's more than just a bod."

I pussyfoot around embarrassed, limply adding, "Organisation's a skill."

"Haf, haf." I'm thumped on the back for that, led haffing into the kitchen where we stand while I watch him operate his ice machine. Miriam joins us, her face newly repaired.

"Where's Ruth?"

"In the bathroom. We're going to move to the halfway hut."

"Aah," Miriam clutches at her throat.

"Aah, I don't believe it, I'd given up. I thought, Well, well I can't go on, I'll just have to lose her. Get me a whiskey, Bill. Hah, she can be just so infuriating."

The fridge opens, chicken comes out, soda, Miriam pours an automatic double.

"I've never known anyone who irritates so effectively and then she stops. Typical Taurean, midsentence and with Scorpio rising—maddening. . . . I couldn't have arranged a more exasperating birth date. The annoying part is she's often right."

Miriam looks, deep glug, into my eyes.

"What's your star sign, Mr. Waters?"

Shit . . . She's waiting, expectant. I loathe star signs, they drive me nuts, I'm more interested in Ruth's rightness.

"Cancer."

"Oh I don't know many Cancers."

"Well I'm one. May I use the bathroom?"

"Helen Keller was a Cancer."

Miriam blows her nose, still red from crying.

"Was she?"

Fake interest, no kidding. Ruth's finally out of the bathroom. As I sit, I can hear Robbie complaining in the kitchen.

"He should have told me, I'm the head of security around here, I mean who's going to secure her down there? Yes? . . . You tell me that?"

Miriam: "I don't know, Robbie, he didn't mention it."

Puss: "No, and he wouldn't have to; it's pretty isolated down there."

Robbie: "Exactly—that's why Stan asked me and Fabio up here."

Puss: "Well, where's she going to run to then?"

Robbie: "Out."

Miriam: "Out where?"

Robbie: "Out to sunbathe."

Miriam: "Put that drink back!"

My eye keeps returning to the razor blades, lying in the vanity cabinet. They nag, so I check them to see if they're releasable, most modern blades are fixed. There's an old model in the cupboard, which I unscrew. The blades look rusty, undisturbed. Good—she won't be cutting . . . obsessive thinking anyway. The cabinet's messy, junk hoarded for no reason, expired medicines, free shampoo samples, no paracetamol (suicide's friend), lotion. I plop some out, my skin's dry.

Three o'clock, mind numbingly hot and Ruth has reenergised. She is sitting cross-legged on the bed, pink cushion on her lap, her face washed and clear.

"Kidnapping is illegal. You're holding me against my will."

"Ruth, we have to go."

No movement, bored sigh.

"What is your will, Ruth?"

Nothing, nasal sigh.

"Are you in control of your will? Could you believe in anything?"

Her hand moves.

"Are you saying my beliefs are crap, are you saying

Baba's crap?" The cushion is plucked, her fingers dig and pull at the staples.

"I'm asking you how your will works."

"I don't really care how it works, it just does. I listen and deduct from a series of propositions."

"So you can control your mind . . ."

Tock, tock, tock, the door taps, opens, it's Fabio.

"Yes," I say.

He says, "I'm here."

I say, "Yes?"

He flicks his head towards the hall, "I'm taking you through."

He assumes an at-ease position, the door couldn't be wider. I put on my sunglasses. Ruth has risen, demanding hers.

"Excuse me?"

"Everybody else here has sunglasses. I need some too."

Fabio's are mirrored, she walks up looking into them.

"Can I have yours, Fabio, I'll bring them back or . . . you could come down and get them?"

That I didn't need so I lent her mine. Fabio stormed a path out front, halting so abruptly before each offending toy, shoe, magazine, I twice banged up against his butt with Ruth piling into mine. A shameful display. I almost tumbled completely over him thinking he wouldn't possibly reach for a sock. Jerk! The family was in the kitchen watching, giggling. The whiskeys clunked down as she approached.

"Well done, dear."

"Yes, good luck, Ruthie."

Ruth stopped, sunglasses bobbing.

"Fuck off will you. All of you."

"You watch yourself, madam," says Gilbert—tall, gold-rimmed glasses, nervous pressed lips. "You watch yourself with your mother."

Ruth's lips twitched back, the walk through wasn't walking.

"Watch myself? Watch myself, SHIT you can talk, what about your secretary's little love bomb, is she happy? Is she living in an ashram? You deceiver!"

Her voice was loud, Gilbert's harsh and thin.

"Don't talk rubbish; she's speaking rubbish."

Miriam touches his arm. "Don't engage with her, Gilly."

Puss whispers, "What love bomb?"

"Hah! He knows." Ruth clicks her tongue.

Gilbert pours another drink. "She's in a complete fantasy."

"Oh I am, am I? Shall we ring her up then."

I pull Ruth forwards.

"Hypocrite. Well he is, I'm fucking sick of it, they don't know what works in life, how could they know what works, they haven't even questioned it. Robots."

I tug her, we're almost out, almost through the door. . . . She stiffens and turns on me. "Take your hands off, Santa."

I do, I apologise. She accepts, not because she wants to, she accepts to stay safe. Muttering, "Cowards, I hate them all. Jingle bells, jingle bells, jingle all the way . . . Hey!—I'd like a nice little house on the prairie, I'd like a nice little car . . . Hey!"

We walked/sang our way out along the clothes line past the emu enclosure. I peered in, I hadn't seen them in the flesh before. Bigger than I thought and very ugly birds, similar to the ostrich with midget heads and darkly bulbous eyes.

Miriam came out dazed and rubbery. Yvonne was at the jeep with Toddy, Toddy was jumping from the hood. He jumped as Yvonne waved to us, so of course she misses him. I couldn't believe it, I kind of blinked through the splat. And for five seconds we four were stunned by him, by Yvonne, by the unbelievably stupid event we'd had to witness. Ruth's shoulders quivered, tempted by the horror hilarity, Toddy wailed, he was winded. Yvonne knelt, knees tucked geisha style, avoiding further damage outfit-wise. Miriam had had it, rigor mortis. Ruth slipped a bangle from her wrist, with great dexterity—it worked on Toddy as a gift.

How we got into the Toyota I do not know, pet kangaroos and enormous sheep butting away at us, this was not New York. I had to go with the flow, and was sick of it. I wanted to go berserk! Fling lists round, demand some "can do." Assuming the can do could be done. The proposition was intensely wearing, my temples pounded with futility. Change what you can, leave what you can't, and have the wisdom to know the difference.

Spent the next ten minutes looking at Ruth, considering the potential difficulties of working on my own. One to one is different, I'm just trying to remember how. More intense because there's nothing to dilute the personalities, and no co-workers, feedback, or respite from continuous pressure. Obviously in that sense it's an issue, "the feedback," better to have the support, but usually I take charge anyway. Okay, it's different, not the ideal situation, but what can I do? Make it work.

The drive to the hut took thirty minutes all on red sand roads. Emus, kangaroos, and cattle, and it was cooking. Real cusp territory, marginal grazing land, more desert than grass. Dried river beds edged with crazed white-limbed gums, many of them leafless, ghost trees.

The hut was simple, clean, on the edge of one of those dead rivers, different from my bug-infested image. It was ten miles from the house. It was 5:08 p.m. Ruth was quiet.

5

I am blank not furious, neutral. Sitting in the familiar hut trying to unpick the day, and decipher what the hell had gone on in India that had got me exposed to all this. If I'd taken a gun to McDonald's I could have understood it. The total flipout, restraints, counsellors, you'd expect it, but ordering a McGod burger's not the same. Unless there's some special inquisition I don't know about, some sin against the state where you're arrested for being involved with anachronistic religious activities. Stuff to no monetary purpose.

It's specially vexing as I'd already explained to Mum in Delhi my path was enlightenment. When I met her off the plane, I asked her how she would feel if I were to become enlightened? I was trying to describe how it was for me the first time with Baba, how I was fretting I wouldn't react to him or couldn't, or that I'd do something dumb and humiliating, like convulse and shatter into tiny glass globules. None of that happened. I was sitting opposite him and we looked and looked—one of his eyes had a blue fleck in it. I laughed. My face felt stiff and nervous wondering what he was seeing there. He stared into the back and the front of me as if he had two focuses—me in my entirety, and me now. I relaxed, then tried to arrange how I wanted him to receive me. He laughed. I knew he knew and I wanted to get up. My hands pushed the ground, my body wouldn't move, his head was nodding. "Ha, ha." I tried again, my insides were going *dope head, get up! GET UP*. His hands danced, thumbs on index finger, "'S good, 's good," and like, *hello*. I'm fully arranged, I can't get up. He puts his hand on mine. I stop and look at my hand as if it's not my hand anymore. I feel very, very relaxed about this, a great surety in the simpleness of me and my hand and his hand on it—suddenly there's nothing to know, except this moment that I am in, until I realise I have never been in a moment, any moment in my whole life, like I am in this moment now. I am not hallucinating, I am in fact de-hallucinating, the world is more absolutely itself than it has ever been and I am struck with the fullness of this inside my chest.

Puffs of pollution and clouds of pungent smells steamed up from the road. In India the sun seems to boil all in its way and steam cook the rest. Animal shit, rotten food scraps, big sputum globules, and mud line the street on each side of the Chatawali Diner, where all of us Westerners hang out because *Lonely Planet*, the bible of all Indian guide books, says we do and so we do.

Mum was telling me Dad was sick, using a Wet One to wipe her straw. I couldn't really figure it out: If he was sick, what was she doing here?

"Hah, well he wanted me to see you and see how you are."

"Can't you tell?"

"Well, you seem happy."

"I am, I'm fantastically happy, Mum."

She wiped her hands before disposing of the tissue in a small brown plastic nappy disposal bag, except she couldn't separate the edges, they were moist from the humidity and had stuck together. Finally she wrapped it in the bag and sucked cautiously on the Diet Coke.

"Dad was thinking you might like to come home with me." A quaky hand was put on mine.

"Ruth, he'd like you to come home."

"Mum, I can't."

"Why?"

"My path is here."

I ordered more chia. Mum kept staring over at this Western couple dressed Oxfam Indian, with a baby. The woman was English, possibly an Honourable Lady Sarah, and her partner was German. Obviously irresponsible flakes. I knew she wanted me to comment, so I didn't because what can you do? The baby was happy and clean, better than going to a boarding school from age seven and having serial nannies before that.

The light in Delhi makes people look lovely. I was looking at Mum, she was so anxious but beneath that the real her looked lovely and pampered and gorgeous. I suddenly felt love for her and wanted to tell her; I knew if I could share the experience properly she would open and flourish. Mum's a flower, a very moist one, she needs to flourish.

"Mum, I'm going to be enlightened."

She heard, she drew herself physically back to me.

"Did you hear what I said? You've got to do it with me."

"Hmmm." Lots of concentration on the straw.

"Well what do you think?"

"About what?"

"About what I said, the enlightenment, the possibility of us doing it together."

"I don't know how it works."

Rustle, rustle, the compact came out and she started to apply lipstick. Baba had taught us how to separate, how you don't have to be tangled in other people's moods. The restaurant looked all wrong, it didn't a minute ago. Now there were flies and stains all over the place.

Mum hissed, "Toilet!" I took her to the hole with two bricks. She said, "Don't be ridiculous," so we headed back to the Hare Hare Hotel with its safe sit-down toilet.

At the hotel she busied herself with the Missing Persons notice board, head nodding, lips moving as she read out Mikal's statistics—beloved daughter 22, 5' 6", 168 cm, light build, last reported travelling north to Dehra Dun, never arrived, last sighting Meerut, Jan. 1997. The hotel manager had now joined her, telling tales of the mother's hapless search.

"She went everywhere, she was joined by the Britishers but, this that this . . ." his hand flapjacked, "she have no luck."

We all peered at the photograph. Mikal had a Streisand nose, brown eyes, long curly hair parted in the middle, full lips. You'd definitely recognise her, among millions you'd recognise her, which Mum pointed out. There were two more Israeli photographs and an English boy from Milton Keynes, he had even features with nose and ear piercings, much harder to find. Indistinct. I sort of wondered where they were as well. Mum asked if they'd been murdered. The manager perked up at this— he loved this sort of disaster talk. "Is possible," he said sucking his lip, "sometimes these people reappear. I saw a boy, stood here looking at himself on the wall and laughing, laughing like a crazy thing. . . . Oh yes, we have to call the ambulance many times, party crowd very bad, dirty boys, very dirty."

Mum was obsessed with beggars, horrible pongs, bottled water, toilet paper, travel pack tissues, cows, and cow shit, despite the fact you don't see much shit as it's constantly recycled into pretty cow pat patterns. There's lots of cows about though. The Indians call them vagabond cows, they don't produce milk, they wander into traffic and eat everything. They're not cute, posing under bougainvillea with legs crossed, they sprawl at random up grass verges onto the motorway, in every other street, park, clump of green. They let you know you're in India and control freaks can piss off. Cows rule India.

Drugs were her other tick. Not heroin, her own. Tea tree oil, Ventolin, Temazepan, Imodium, Betnovate, Voltarol, Anadin, Beconase, TCP, antibiotics—Paludraine, Avloclor. And diseases, when we travelled to Rishikesh she refused everything and this is going executive on the train, her insistence. I ate like a pig.

Mum is after cheap grace. She wants something for nothing, that's basically what crystal twirling and horoscope readings do for you, strokes and pats, reassurance and you don't ever have to confront anything basic about yourself or your life. She loved two things about India: textiles and *The Hindustan Times*, the matrimonials, their keenness for horoscopes: blah blah suitable match for fair, beautiful, homely Brahmin girl, 23/160 MBA and well versed in domestic chores. Qualified professionals with similar background preferred. Write with bio-data horoscope. Early decent marriage. Box 120300. Blah, babble. Wanted: virgin pharmacist for Punjabi chemist, blah. Wanted: innocently divorced, public school, caste no bar, convent educated, five-figure salary, MBA, B.Ed., BE, CA, MMC, M.Com., M.Sc. (physic).

Rishikesh divides into two, Hell rubble town and Candyland, separated by the Ganges. When we arrived, I plonked her down at the rooftop cafe in Candyland. She balked a bit when she saw the white-faced, tubby Guru at the entrance. I told her the Beatles had eaten here, which impressed her, placed her in the middle away from the monkeys and left to get Rahi. Rahi is older, Western, and very calm.

Mum's first words to Rahi were about Dad. Rahi breathed in empathy as Mum revealed the true extent of his illness. Why hadn't I had the gory details? She said she'd tried to tell me in Delhi, but had felt unsupported, head coyly held to one side. Rahi massaged her shoulders.

"Yes, he's very ill, they think he had a stroke at Puss's farm and he won't be moved, he's still up there."

I said, "What?" but I'd heard, Mum knew I'd heard, we often did that "what?" business, a kind of family habit where we run into reruns, I don't know why, and I didn't know what to say either. Sometimes I get overly blunt when I'm feeling the opposite.

"God, is he going to die?"

Mum sniffs. "It's possible, the doctors don't know yet. Ruth, he wants to see you, he's bought the ticket home for you."

"Oh, Mum." My hand rubs hers. "Poor Daddy, maybe next time."

This is in reference to the karmic wheel, which she doesn't get, and starts to huff.

"But we've got your ticket for you."

Blah. We argue about the ticket, which I can't pay for. She says they're paying, but I don't want them to. It's not a matter of their conniving, it's the silent barter, which works: you pay or perform and that's fair, not necessarily honest. And I want to be honest and stop walking round zzzing in this fucking maze conversation where we add up all the little unsaid words till we somehow know we've got to the centre. Which is what?

And then there's the initiation.

Rahi: "Umm it's really the timing isn't it, Nazni?"

Mum: "Who is Nazni?"

Rahi: "Nazni's Ruth, it's her apprentice name."

Mum: "Ruth, can you speak for you?"

Me: "I'd really rather you call me Nazni, it's my name now. . . ." (Visible breath from Mum.) "You see they only initiate new sannyasins once a year and it happens to be next week."

"Fine. You are doing just as you should. You are pleasing yourself, which is exactly what we brought you up to do. No, you go and please yourself, don't let our deaths inconvenience you."

A tear trickles down my face. "Okay."

I feel completely overwhelmed, so does Mum. There's not much in my life I have really wanted to go for. I can't tell her I love Chidaatma Baba eternally, much more than my own family, but I do. We have a complete understanding. I can place myself in his heart, mentally, and there is absolutely nothing he has to worry about concerning me. My behaviour towards him will never change. He has shown me capacities I didn't think I had, they were dead.

"I'm sorry, I can't go back, Mum."

"Ruth, what if he dies?"

"I hope he won't."

That's the best I can manage; it's not enough. Rahi steps in, she takes Mum to one side and I hear her whispering. Oh, what now, what now? Mum comes back, her arm around Rahi, she'll visit Baba.

"It's a beautiful opportunity, Miriam, Baba will be taking questions."

Baba doesn't allow people with perfume or body odour to enter the ashram. Back at our villa, Rahi and Priya rinse Mum's blouse six bloody times—I can hardly bear it. Finally we get to the gates.

"Ruth, I can't go through with this."

"Why?"

"I feel like an animal."

"Have a look, you'll see it's beautiful, the food's good."

We shuffle forward in segregated lines of men and women. Chants are playing through rusty tin loudspeaker systems bolted to the outside wall in cages. Money, money, money, a tall thin boy complains to a fifty-year-old American woman with a dishevelled hennaed ponytail. She talks about the Celestine Prophecy, how you have to watch for signs—army men behaving badly, planting dope. "They were inhuman." She doesn't feel she can invite her cousin now, she wants to discuss it all with Baba. A taxi load of Western devotees drives to the front and is stepped aside for. A Japanese hippy couple are having an argument, nobody but Mum takes any notice. As one more person ahead fails the scent test, Mum steps out of line, "I can't, I can't be sniffed at, I'm going back." Her throat blotches.

"No, come on, you can do it, just walk with me."

We push on through. Everyone is chanting, up ahead are life-sized casts of Baba's feet, people queuing for the hall are bowing and kissing them, leaving offerings, sweets, marigolds, a piece of apple cake. I pass a yellow flower to Mum, who gives a little shudder.

"You don't have to kiss them."

"No, don't touch me. I'm not coming."

She shrugs my arm off, I try to keep hold of her, people look on in bliss, they seem to make her shrugs more violent.

"No!"

"All right. Well, wait for me at my villa, you can rest on my bed."

"Your mattress."

"All right, mattress."

Her tone is spiteful. She demands to be taken back to her hotel.

"Mum, I can't. I have to go in."

"I'm asking you, Ruth."

God! I snap and snap. My exasperation levels soar,

emotional wobble, just bloody knew she'd do this. I want it, she knows I want it, she doesn't want it, but she doesn't want me to have it. Shit!

"What's the matter? You know where our villa is, it's only a street back."

"I can't lie on that floor."

She's sweating, we look at each other, hate . . . she's breathing heavily. Neither of us move. I say, "Okay, well ring me." Christ!

I didn't see, but Mum was crying. She got all tizzed up by a small mob of rickshaw drivers and hawkers, she'd bought water from one, which is not a good thing to do, can spark a kind of frenzy, which it did. She tried to escape down a lane without the rickshaw driver, he followed anyway, then she lost her shoe, which set some children off quarrelling and asking for rewards, she got agitated with no small change on her, only one hundred rupee notes. She looked in her bag for the asthma spray, which everybody thought was reward money and drove her madder with demands. The spray wasn't there anyway, it was back at the bloody hotel. The handbag signalled more and more people, her breathing deteriorated. She kept saying, "It's at the hotel, it's at the hotel."

No one understood what the "it" was, so more people came jostling and knocked her down. She knocked herself down, crawling out on all fours hugging the handbag, and was passed unconscious over everybody's head into the back of a taxi. Her money wasn't even stolen.

End of India. She had a bad, bad, asthma attack. She'd brought her own needle, but she couldn't explain she wanted the needle picked up from her hotel room, so she began panicking about AIDS, hepatitis A, B and C, and became even more thorough with the baby wipes so that everything, her knife, fork, spoon, glass, hands, smelled foul with that poxy sweet freshener that immediately reminds me of baby pooh. The Embassy insisted I accompany her back to Sydney. She was hydraulically lifted into the 747 where we took up five seats, three for her, one for me and one for her saline drip and her oxygen tank.

Fate, I felt, was taking me home. After all there must be something I had to say to my father—yeah: "Fuck you Father for what I'm about to receive."

I'm sitting in an old leather armchair watching Bill Bill spray the hut for bugs. PJ isn't with us, he's unpacking in his room. I can hear intermittent scrapy noises, coat hangers against steel. There are two bunk rooms, mine has twin beds, his has a large single. Plastic sheets are being removed—I begin to feel guilty—I'm not removing them, not being industrious. Tim helps Bill Bill, no one says anything. No one even looks at me, I must beam out "difficult person," expect no helpee, helpee. I jig my bare foot. He'd asked for my shoes on the way down, so he got them, given on automatic pilot, rude not to. Felt good about it at the time, mindless blurry action.

Why am I being so passive? Sitting here saying, "Yes, do it to me." Usually you sort of know what's in store for you. Apart from the Baba experience, I can usually guess.

If Baba were here now, they'd all be surrendering. My worst moment was telling him I had to go. I decided to wear my uninitiated, initiation robes, it just felt like the right thing to do. I went in, knelt down, kissed his feet, stood up, and said goodbye. Then I turned away and, well, punched my head so violently he had to come over and hold me.

"Would you like tea?" says Mr. Big Dude Waters.

"Yes I would like some tea, with milk, thank you."

Everybody's gone. I sit here, sipping tea, watching PJ, the scary joke, playing Mum. He has a lot of lines when he smiles, they're not fleshy, they disappear when he stops. He's a wee bit sweaty. I can't decide if he has bandy legs or not, they're worse from the back. I sort of flash myself a series of warning flashcards: "Be polite," "Don't act loony," "Chill."

"Did you like Sydney?"

"Yes thank you, it's very lush. Were you born there?"

"Just out. In Cronulla, past the airport, it's a beach town. Lots of children and hosties—airport people. Have you been to Australia before?"

"No, and actually what I want to talk about is you, Ruth."

"Uh-huh, yeah . . . Well, when I was eight we used to come down here and play with Gary the farmhand. He was a huge bloke and he wouldn't talk to us. He pulled us along on his trailer, actually pulled it himself with a rope. Once he cut open a dead ewe with two miniature lambs inside her, they were so white in this blue sac, transparently white, I wanted to touch them. I had my hand out, stretched out to the blue sac when he kicked them into a hole."

PJ's cup goes down. The memory makes me feel odd, seeing those lambs and the sloshing sound their bodies made in that hole.

"He probably wasn't safe, he was too lonely, poor guy, he killed himself drinking sheep dip." I look up. "Have you ever been suicidal?" Mr. Waters stares at me, there's an uncomfortable pause, he hardly moves, which makes me fidget more—all I get is a "No."

A nonhumorous "No." I drink, thinking spas, I'm not sticking this. He's just trying to head fuck me. That sort of thing where the other person remains passive and you're the dick. You do all the talking while they look, they haven't really got anything to say but they look superior. I yawn.

"How was Sydney?"

He snorts. "You've asked me that. You know I don't want to talk about Sydney."

"Well I do."

"Well I don't. I want to concentrate on you now."

He's leaning in, hands on knees. I'm trying not to look with any particular look. The room's getting darker and thicker, I want to go.

So I say, "Look this isn't going to work because we're too different. I don't think I'm capable of appreciating your position."

I stand, he doesn't move.

"Well," I say. "I think I'll go and lie down now."

I don't wait, I leave. One thing I can usually do is take action; action infuriates other people because as soon as you move you're not them. The instant you shift you're you.

Relief. The bedroom door actually shuts. Phew, I turn the pillow over, no creepy-crawlies. I dump down on my front, I'll sleep the three days. Then I notice there's no fan in here, he's got the only fucking fan. Ohhh shit. I'm not going out there, I'm not going to go and negotiate with him. My nose is blocked, I lie on my back, the room's depressing, one window behind my head. I stare at the ceiling, thinking empty ceiling thoughts.

6

5:40 p.m. Second tantrum. The only thing that vaguely pisses me off is the heat, it's sticky, I don't like to feel sticky. I prefer cool. Age might have something to do with it, nobody warned me.

Ruth is not the piss-off she imagines herself to be, that's not to say she isn't a piss-off, because she is. I'm trying to keep the games right down so I can see who is pissing who. I could have reacted more to her sheep dip story, my no play could have been misinterpreted as callous, which it probably was, but we both know we're not here to discuss sheep dip. The thing is with this kind of family, the jokey type, my tone has to be different. I say that and of course can see contradictions with this, what's another clown matter? I could entertain that, see that working but I've never been that funny. I can be cute, sarky-funny, according to Carol . . . whom I keep forgetting to call. I doubt the mobile's capacity, time differences, and feel uncomfortable leaving Ruth in a state of triumph. She's not so much in the situation as over it, active types do that, they fear immersion, feeling paralysis lies round the corner. So where's this ding-a-ling revelation getting me: not far enough.

But I have the only fan and plug it in. We almost had a conversation going back at the farmhouse, control of the mind. She was listening, Fabio shattered it. I don't want to go straight back in on that tack or she'll think there's some kind of set program or we'll get into nonproductive police state arguments. It's called right action; to take no action would be bad, to take inflexible action would be equally bad.

For three minutes I put my face in the fan, bliss. Next I walk heavily towards her door, I want her to know I'm coming. I knock, wait, open the door. She's on the bed, jumps off it, walks over, and slams the door—bang, fine, I get a chair. Same procedure, knock, wait, open the door, she leaps up, it won't close because I've wedged a chair in the doorway. Outcome: polite conversation.

"Excuse me!"

"Excuse me what?"

"Your chair's blocking the doorway and I want to lie down."

"I know, I'm sorry, but I'm going to require a bit more from you than this." I sit astride the chair.

In case it's not obvious I'm going to continue, I quickly do so. I say, "God is potentially an interesting subject."

This produces a throw yourself on the bed fit, hands over her ears, face into the pillows, wah wah noises as loud as she can go. I expect rebellion, I'm prepared for it.

"That's fine. I didn't expect it to be easy, you're an intelligent young lady with strong convictions, it would be a little disappointing if you were too quick."

She didn't hear me she was wah wahing so much, feet drumming the mattress, spurts of dust shooting out.

I cough.

"Questioning is ultimately about courage. How well do you know your material?"

"Ha, ha, ha . . ." from the bed.

I flick a handkerchief around dispersing dust.

"We could start with God as product: who's making who? Are we making God or is God making us? Or are we just participating in endless projections? What do you think, Ruth?"

She laughs, "Ha, ha, ha," her hands slip from her ears. I'm told to shut up, and don't.

"'The pure heart seeks beyond intellect, it gets inspired.' What about that, Ruth? You like that?"

Ruth resumes her ha, ha, ha, shut up mantra.

Boring. My legs get stiff. I begin again, not absolutely sure where we were.

"Which one of these sayings belongs to Baba, Ruth? Did he say 'The pure heart seeks beyond intellect,' or was it 'The mind is a propeller, you turn it off and still it keeps flapping, flapping?'"

There's a lull on the mattress then a heave, followed by another heave.

"Ha ha ha, shut up. Ha ha ha, shut up." (The second ha ha ha was muffled.)

"Finished?"

"Ha ha ha, shut up."

"Thank you."

"Ha ha ha, shut up."

I wait. Her face is in the mattress.

"Or did he say . . . or did he say, 'For the self to be reborn you must find a master to cleanse you of all social and political conditioning. Only the master can remove the blockage, your own attachment will be too great.'"

I get a "shit" and a flush-faced Ruth sits up abruptly and abruptly delivers a nasty titbit about my hair. She says there's no way she can even listen to someone like me who uses hair dye.

My hand touches my hair—involuntary response—it reaches up and lightly touches thin wet hair. She doesn't see this, anyway she doesn't comment, I do. I say, "That's pretty superficial."

Her feet swing onto the floor. A little bit of pacing goes on beside the bed. She didn't like the *superficial,* I could tell—it pushed her own bitchy little hair comment back in her face.

"So which one was Baba's?" There's a pause. I don't allow it. "Can you guess? Come on, you know his teachings, don't you?"

Ruth jams elbows onto knees, fists into cheeks. Deep contemplation produces, "Can I have my shoes back?"

This is plain stubborn and could be an act, there's no co-worker to check against so I say no.

"No, you agreed to stay down here and I'm going to make it easy. There's going to be no temptation."

There's a big sigh. "This is annoying me."

"It must be very annoying for you and it will be annoying for you. . . ."

"No! You are annoying me."

My feet ease out of the doorway, toes wriggling back circulation. Ruth hears my boots squeaking and rolls round to look at what's squeaking, or pretends to, her face looks a little different, hard to judge in this light. She says, "The thing is, I don't care what you say. I have the right to the spirituality of my choice."

"You have."

"Well good," she says, very cheery, "let's go home," jumps up and walks round the room, repeating, "Let's go home, let's go home."

"Just sit down, please." She doesn't, I continue. "You have the right to the spirituality of your choice. Absolutely. That's not the issue. The issue is the meaning of that word choice and whether you had one."

She tells me she has made a choice, the choice chose her. I ask if she'd mind if we moved and had a cup of tea in the other room. Predictably she does. So, I try another angle, "Well that sounds firm, tell me what is your mind, and how do you make it up? Is it like a bed, you can change it with a sheet? Or is it hard and solid like a brick?"

All the time I'm quietly backing out of the room, as close to nonacknowledgement as you can get, "So is it thick as a brick, always the same rain or shine, nothing gets through?" I see the light switch and want to turn it on but don't, fearing I'll break whatever invisible threads we've strung between us.

"Do you only have the thoughts you want to have? Like if I say to you don't think of pink elephants, you don't, right, or do you?"

She walks on ahead of me into the middle of the living room.

"It's a game, the pink elephant stuff, it's just a game."

"You just mentioned them."

Her eyelids tighten. "Ho, ho."

"You see, your mind is a rebel, not a servant. I'm not the one who will break you Ruth, your own mind will. 'It will seek the truth and the truth will set you free.' John 8:32."

I turn the light on. She tells me I forced her to think pink, now she sees a pink halo. She tells me my nose has grown a pink elephant trunk, her hand acts out an elephant trunk with snuffly accompaniment. The trunk snuffles to the tea, which is picked up in a complicated way, hand twisted and turned under.

"Your elephant nose looks like a penis."

I ignore penis bullshit, her trunk snorts at my ear.

"Is that why you escaped to India: jokey, jokey family?"

More trunk snorting, away from me this time, snuffling round the windowsills, dead flies are brushed to the floor. Snort, snort, the trunk waves towards me, poises midair and breaks up at the sight of me, my nose sends her off completely. She ha hahs all over herself, clasps hands, bends double, continues snuffling. So, I repeat myself: "Is jokey family why you escaped to India?"

She's says she's too busy and can't be bothered answering such a boring question.

I watch and fantasise the trials of living with a family in denial. Would I like it? Why wouldn't I like it? I wouldn't like it if I were unfortunate enough to think. I was tempted to add scientifically, philosophically, or psychologically, but just plain "think" will do. Instant sensation, gratification. Feel hungry, pick in the fridge; bored, pick at the shops, the TV, the phone, the dope—purchasable items that don't require cerebral interaction . . . humour giving the illusion something's *going on*. This is put to Ruth. Increasing snort activity by several decibels.

7

The trouble with elephant imitating is, it's too engross-ing, you just want to wave your trunk 'round and drop it on people's heads. Or pull houses down—that would be quite satisfying—bonking out walls. Their trunks are so bloody strong, you can feel the potential flexing, subtle hints of it, a friendly squeeze before the trainer yells some elephant warning and the trunk relaxes your hand. There's that moment when you wonder if you'll be seen as another mammal or something to swat at. None of us tested ourselves that much in Jaipur. We watched the trainer sway lovingly with the trunk, staggering off balance as he was pooped up and down. The trust you'd have to have, the trunk wrapped 'round my wrist said it all. The temptation to squeeze the big mass with its oh-so-small, vulnerable eyes. I didn't know how you could do it though, boss them about. Whether you had to dominate them as a trainer or completely surrender to them. I couldn't accept that they could be compliant to some-one my size.

The hut has yellowy-brown hills out the front, not terribly high, about four rows of them. If I knew the precise distance I could calculate. At a guess, at least a kilometre from here. The snuffling has become part of a shoe search, an unsuccessful one. Unless you count flies. The paint 'round these windows is so flaky, just sits on the wood in scabs, my trunk hoovers through fragments, snorting itself out the window. You couldn't walk to those hills without shoes, not with all the thorns, stones, and bull ants, your feet would be pulp.

I'm still seeing bloody pink elephants, I had a whole herd of them running 'round at one point, proved his point. Ha, ha, penis nose. Penis nose, vagina mouth. The attractive young woman, old hag experiment, where we had to look at silhouettes and say what we saw. Most people saw the pretty young thing in profile, but I saw an old woman with a pointed nose. Once the teacher revealed the double aspect you couldn't help flipping between the two. That's what PJ's guilty of, seeing only the one aspect.

I can't go back to the farmhouse anyway. Dad hates me even more now. Mum gets me to do this, say the unspeakable, the things that no one wants to bloody well hear, well they do but in secret. She must like the shock, some sort of payback revenge. The thing is, Mum always tells me these things, forgets she's said them or alluded to them, and then feigns innocence when I bring them up. I'm not a good secret-keeper, which is why I'm told. I still don't know much about this half sister, apart from the fact that she's the result of one of Dad's pathetic affairs. Apparently she's blonde and lives in Brisbane.

I go over and snuffle PJ's hair, which is damp and lanky. Not exactly attractive, in fact mildly disgusting. I go purrt purrt through it anyway, which is supposed to sound like an elephant. He jerks his head away and sets his face. I purrt purrt back. His hand flicks out at mine, he gives a little nod.

"Can we cut down the funnies, Ruth?"

"Oh come on, what am I supposed to do?"

"Confront yourself, confront your beliefs."

This is given heavy, heavy weight: expectation. At some level, I must be susceptible to "heavy"; it sets off a dull excitement in me. I don't really know if it's beyond or below the trivial me, it's the raw me. Whatever it is it's very intense, a sort of passion of closeness similar to a confession with no distance. I've tried to talk about it but found misunderstandings made me seem mad. I believe there's another door through disintegration into euphoria and that maybe only a woman can get there. I was starting to get there with Baba.

The thrill of something about to happen, I don't know what he really wants . . . but I know how to make things happen. I just have to blurt stuff out. It's sort of sledgehammer stuff, but it works.

"You know my father and brother are cunt men."

I wait a second for this to trickle through, his eyes look at me, no change of expression. "Yes, they believe in porno magazines, they just can't get enough smut. Girls in natural surroundings, health camps, waterfalls. Robbie likes hardcore, he thinks hardcore sex is a great belief."

I bloody near bite my cheek off with this . . . especially the waterfalls, ha, ha, ha. He doesn't answer immediately, he sort of ponders the floor.

"Do you know what your guru's really asking you to do?"

"Have sex with him?"

"Well . . . no, he's asking you to leave your brain behind . . . and all other influences."

"Can I get myself a drink?"

"Of course you can."

"Do you want one?"

"No."

A bad thing happens at the fridge, I pull the water out and the whole plastic shelf thing holding the milk and other drinks comes with it. The trouble is, I practically get a giggle fit with the smut stuff. It's this bloody awful memory of Mum's friend Deborah coming to stay in Robbie's room and shifting junk about to put her clothes away and setting off this avalanche of porn. Nearly knocked her out. Fuck—I just can't control myself, I sort of pretend I'm looking for things in the fridge, snorting, and have to trunk-snuffle louder to shut myself up. I can't seem to calm down. PJ's taking no notice, which is crap because he must have heard me.

PJ is sitting with his cowboy boots on the coffee table, he sees me and pats a cushion. God, I'm not sitting down on a patted cushion . . . so I go 'round in a circle practising mindful walking where you place one foot slowly in front of another saying *om*. The *om* goes a bit quavery, which sounds feeble and trembly, so I have to hum.

"Sit down," he says.

I don't sit down. He can't make me.

8

6:22 p.m. Ruth blurred in front of me, her circle narrowing. Saris expose the midriff, is the thought, plus how to stick my head in a bucket of water. I have sweat on my eyebrows, ears, upper lip, neck area, and generally everywhere. I was hoping she'd tire, at least I might get physical clues. The fact is I can't put too much on the sit, because I can't make her sit, all these suggestions have to be very neutral, presented as an open possibility— "sit down," it's as if I'm giving Ruth permission to allow herself to sit. She didn't, she may later when she has digested and made the suggestion her own. You play out these little strategies, they work, they don't work, you can't get chewed out by them. She hasn't been much better in the living room, slowing down only marginally. Selfish, selfish, selfish.

One thing, very few people with brains can be bastards or bitches forever, goes against the grain. No matter how dominant the current identity is there's nearly always a head battle about what the authentic identity's doing underneath. For all her buoyancy this matters to her. She's not quite sure where the real her is, or if she's representing a "her" far, far away from the original.

And here she comes with a bottle of water and no glasses, honk, honk, greetings from the chronically self-obsessed. She swigs as she walks towards, not especially me, but my end of the room, without caring how the hips go. The face isn't all even, the eyes aren't fantastic blue orbs, they have an almond shape sloping upwards with gray-blue irises. Strong eyebrows, strong lips. What's more attractive is the energy pumping out, elevates her into another category of the extremely noticeable.

She looks damn near an amber goddess, with the low sunlight tinting red—it accentuates the hairs on her skin, padding her out so she doesn't quite end where her skin ends. You don't get the Audrey Hepburns these days, the fragility isn't there, certainly isn't there on the exterior, women have muscles now.

She sits, puts the water bottle almost on top of my boots.

"Do you want me to remove them?"

"Yes, it's rude."

"It is, I have a sore hip."

"Well, leave them then."

"Thank you, I'll leave one."

I point to the water. "May I?" She passes the bottle, which has a condensed filmy dew, my hands slip. I have to take my legs off the table and adjust myself so I can pour water out over my handkerchief. She's watching, arms folded, chin in, water trickles out on the floor. I wipe my face, neck, and hands. I take a while with this, she took a while, she can cooperate when she wants to, when there's something to satisfy.

I look at her and think, was I ever that self-absorbed? Yes, according to Carol. *Yes!* She maintains I'm needy, constantly distracting her from Christ knows what . . . something very important like "herself," she says. She calls it my *perpetual dominate theme*—PDT—which assumes right of way over all other themes. Character trait of the seriously deranged: Hitler, Napoleon, Pol Pot. I wasn't really accepting her dogmatic vision of me until the woman who counselled me died and I got my correspondence back.

Dear Jean,

Thank you for your phone call, a lot of these flus seem to be a bi-product of animal–human proximity.

I've been away on an intervention with a Boston family, the son a member of the Hare Krishna, quite poignant. His conversion tied in with the death of his girlfriend who died in a car accident, car driven by him. I ended up going to her grave with him, it affected me in a strange way. He lay across the grave and sobbed. I tried to contain the situation but couldn't, the noise was indescribable. I don't know what else to say, I'm empty of saying as I have so much to do at the moment, and think it best to say goodbye at this point and allow some other person the opportunity of working with you.

Warm regards—PJ

Dear PJ,

Thank you for your beautiful card showing the rain forest in Ecuador, perhaps you picked it up on an excursion with Carol. It was dear of you to send me a card with such growth in view of your ending our meetings. You make clear you do not want to speak about the Krishna case, but I want to tell you how deeply it moved me to read your words about it and how painful it must have been. In Rilke's words, 'Of death we only knew what all men know; That he seizes us and flings us into wordlessness.'

I would like to think that I can be here for you when you should need it, if you should need it in order to—yes—talk it over. I am still struggling with this flu.

    With much love—Jean.

How I could have thought her letter lacked emotion I can't say but when I got it, I honestly felt it did. Mine was a post-card of fucking Ecuador, no particular reference to anything, to her or any of our time together. How she manages to scrape out 'growth' from it slays me. I thought I'd written an incredibly internalised emotional account and Jean was the one who couldn't extend herself to anyone.

Ruth is looking at me without hostility, which is welcome, mediocre, bland. I used to find hostility a turn-on but it's petty. You know you hold all the cards, so what.

"Okay, I'm going to ask you a question. I want to know what in your opinion is the most important task of a human life?"

She picks stray hairs off her sari, examines them, watches them float to the floor.

"Any idea?"

"Is this a multiple choice?"

"Nope, it's an oratory technique. You heard of Socrates?"

She pulls up straight, crossing her legs; I get a cautious, "Yeah."

" 'The soul takes nothing with her to the other world but her education and culture and these it is said are of the greatest service or of the greatest injury to the dead man at the very beginning of his journey thither.' So let's get to the facts. What is Chidaatma Baba teaching you?"

"What's the point of my telling you, you already have an opinion."

A hair is plucked from her head and carefully run through her fingers.

"The point is something's touched you and I want to know what it is. To find that out you'd have to look into my heart, into the 'It is' of it, way beyond something you can read in a book and quote. 'It is,' that's his teaching. 'It is.'"

"Uh-huh." I keep my voice even. "That's what he said? 'It is?' His words?"

Ruth talks to the hair: "His words."

"'He alone attains unto it who exclaims It is! It is! Thus may it be perceived and apprehended in its essence.' The Upanishads, Ruth, The Upanishads."

"Yes, so." She looks up. "I don't care. Who are they anyway?" Left foot starts to jig.

"'They,' Ruth, are a book, an ancient Vedic text. Even Bhagwan Shree Rajneesh, the great example of 'truth stumbling in the marketplace' (Isaiah 59:14), attributed sources. Feel with your heart, but check your texts."

Left foot engages lower body.

"You can't stand the fact that I've got faith, can you? Because you're so frightened and dried up, defending yourself with your textbooks and all your bloody sources, that feeling, just trusting your heart is beyond you and without that you can't love, you can't know anything."

She's up and pacing again, I can hear "Baa Baa Black Sheep" sung deadpan, tuneless. I wait, after a few minutes she sits.

I go in again: "So it doesn't worry you that you have absolutely no knowledge of the texts that form the basis of all Eastern religious philosophy?"

Ruth swings her feet up on the couch and stuffs the cushion I'd patted under her arm.

"I can't remember."

"Well what do you meditate on?"

"Things Baba gives us to meditate on."

"Such as what?"

"Such as . . . the obvious things we all screw up on."

"What are they?"

"They're the obvious things, I don't have to quote them, I don't care whether I remember them or not. Baba's Baba. He's not about texts, he's about experience, that's the whole point. Plenty of arseholes can read, it's just people blahing on without feeling. Big deal, hooray, they can have it. They can stuff it up their computers."

"You're a perfect zombie then, aren't you?"

Her eyes open extra wide, similar to a cat's, except a cat's pupils do all the changing. With Ruth it's the muscles round the eyes that stretch.

"That's right, I'm the perfect zombie."

"You are, aren't you. Mr. and Mrs. Baba tie the knot, she doesn't know what he's saying. He's glad she doesn't. All he has to do is squeeze out a bit of everyday Indian philosophy, because you haven't heard the metaphysical principles of soul and matter."

Ruth puts the cushion under her feet, this is done deliberately and slowly.

"Well?"

"You're annoying me again."

"Why?"

"Look you can't destroy what I know, because I felt it

inside. Okay? You don't seem to get the point. Not everything's a posture, not everything's a bloody charade. When he saw me he saw all of me. To be seen like that . . . it's a privilege, it's total love."

Her eyes are on me without embarrassment, I'm to understand that this is truth. She moves her hand in a clawing motion along the table. A halfhearted attempt to resume elephant snorting.

I sit back, watching her intently.

"Yep, that Total Love's an interesting concept . . . 'You have to have a lot of Love in your heart to do what I did to Tate.' That's what one of those Manson girls said after she'd butchered Sharon Tate's baby."

"Ho, ho, ho."

Ruth has doubled over, both hands near her feet, giggling.

"Ho, ho, ho."

"You find that funny?"

She doesn't answer, continues giggling. When she eventually sits up she kind of groans.

"It's ridiculous."

"Yes it is ridiculous, ripping out a pregnant woman's baby is ridiculous."

"Oh, it's just ridiculous, your whole story, I could never kill a baby."

"Sharon begging for the life of her child, begging these women to spare her unborn baby. But they just couldn't do it, they had to go on and stab her anyway, dip their hands in her blood and other people's blood and write 'pig' and other obscenities on the walls, or was it doors? I can't remember."

"Look!" Ruth's body snaps bolt upright.

"Yes! Look. What *was* going on?"

"Look. Shut up! I don't know what you're talking about, I'm not killing any babies—so you can just fuck off. I'm not listening to this."

"So Manson means nothing to you?"

"I'm not interested."

"So you get the point?"

"No I don't."

"The Manson cult, Charles Manson, guru in the sixties, dedicated followers become knife-wielding maniacs?"

"I've heard of it."

"Then you get the point."

"No, I don't, I don't know the details, I wasn't even born. You can't get into crap like that and accuse me of it. . . ."

"I didn't say it was you. I said it was 'Total love.'"

8:02. The floor scuffs, we both spring apart. Spontaneously combustible, fed-up intermission. She goes out to the toilet, I fill the basin with cold water. I can't wait, my hands plunge in, the veins on my hands have swollen to a delta, tributaries feeding springs. Then I hold my nose and dunk my whole head under.

Ruth spreads out on the floor, palms to ceiling. I go outside and pull my half of the chicken to bits. Fallen morsels of meat are rushed at by ants, big as your thumb nail. The sun is setting. Everything is red and warm. Bar a crow who plops in from nowhere, huge mangy bird with a black beak.

Back inside, and she's sitting cross-legged in a chair, hot drink in hand. I sit opposite, listening to her sip. I'm used to a lot of noise and find the absence of motorised hums, faxes, and answering machines almost unnerving. . . . Her composure looks energetic so I'm waiting for her to deliver something not nice.

"I have decided I'm not going to do the three days."

"Have you?"

"Yes."

"You're a pain."

"I know. And, I also want to say I have been listening to you and I have to tell you something."

She drinks. The "and" here means she may do the three days, the remaining two and a half, on the condition of, let's say (because people like her always have conditions), of, let's say, I shut up and listen to her lecture, I lay off Manson, schlock tabloid, I wimp out and come under her control. She wouldn't want that either, of course, controlling people never do know precisely what it is they do want. They can't believe anybody can give them anything they haven't already mentally deduced as that person's lot, their contribution. Well, I'm going to be the big surprise.

I'm looking at her with renewed feelings of composure, warm sensations running up my body.

Ruth is throat clearing.

"Baba doesn't want that sick sort of devotion. He doesn't want people surrendering to him. He wants you to . . . to surrender to yourself."

"Yeah, well you do, too, don't you, but it's kind of manipulated, isn't it? Curious it doesn't seem to happen to people living in their own homes. Far more likely to happen to people living in a closed community. Where you've got a whole emotional highball going on, people coughing up the past, confessing, counter-confessing."

I have her attention. The sun has gone so there aren't any escape routes out the windows.

"Well, was it freely given?"

"What?"

"You know what I'm talking about, the surrender."

"Ough," she snorts at me. "Ough. Look, I wasn't even wanting it. He just happened to be there sitting in front of me. When I opened my eyes he was sitting there meditating in front of me and he spoke to me. He said, 'How was that?' And I said, 'I saw some light.' He said, 'Did you really?' And I said, 'No.'"

She shrugs like she wants to shrug off the depth and wriggle into now.

"Sorry, what I meant was . . . you weren't living in a neutral space. Baba's Ashram is dedicated to him, all the air for miles around is polluted with Baba bliss.

He materialises trinkets, you hear this, he gave so and so something, you hear that. They come to you in a big whisper, 'Psst, I can't explain . . .' blissed out expression, devotee's head to one side . . . 'oh dear, how to express it.' Your mind doodles with all these stories. He wasn't an anonymous person, you weren't sitting down having a cappuccino with a nobody were you? It's a near hysterical state."

Ruth is leaning forward, pulling at her sari, exaggerating the hysterical.

"I wasn't hy—hy—hysterical,"—said like hiccups—"I was there, I felt it, okay? For Chrissake I tell you my experience and you tell me I didn't have one. What do you want? I can say anything, you don't care, do you? So long as there's something being said you don't care. This is a nuthouse."

"Is it?"

"Yes."

"Could you kill yourself for Baba?"

"I'd like to think I could."

"Is that a rational thought?"

"Yes, because he wouldn't ask me."

"He asked you to marry him, didn't he? Was that a comment on your spirituality or on your beauty?"

She's scratching some bite on her arm, pinching the skin together over the lump, leaves a red impression through the middle. She looks at me looking.

"When you look at me, would you mind looking at my face please."

"Excuse me?"

"When you looked at me then, you were looking at my breasts. I'd prefer it if you looked at my face."

Bang. That kicked in. Of course I did nothing but look at them again—my pink elephants. I was looking in the general area, but not especially, well, obviously her breasts are stuck to the front of her and unavoidable in that sense. I don't go for body parts usually, I purposely try to vary my gaze: person, person in the room, table, floor, eyes. Carol's mumblers were the last body parts to mesmerise, these tight, tight, pants where the lips were moving with nothing coming out. So irrelevant—but I'm not accepting the entire derailment.

"What's frightening you, Ruth?"

"Nothing's frightening me, I just don't want you looking at my breasts."

"I didn't think I was."

"Not all the time but some of the time you were looking at my breasts."

I laughed, she didn't, she was enjoying herself.

"All right. If you feel I was looking at your breasts, I'll make a special effort not to."

I didn't think I'd exactly been targeting them, so part of me wanted to yak on, defending, myself. The observation had been taken from her position, not the only position in the room. It was kind of punitive; okay, I'd acquiesced, okay, I'd made myself less defensive, which was good. Laid down with the bear, didn't fight—just fell down, a toe-curling pussy-whipped rug.

We sit, who's going to be making the move?

Uh-oh, we have action. Ruth's taken herself through to the kitchen area, sari tucking, fully aware that I'm watching. The fridge is opening, the tap is on, a lettuce breaks apart. Concentrated cuts, her entire body is steady, thinking.

Mine has a film of moisture, begging for a shower. Will she stay? She'll do what she'll do, I can't chain her up. This is why we work in pairs—to prevent this sort of situation. I must shower, I get up and tell her. Her eyes are impossible to read, she wants me to worry, she doesn't want me to worry, it's all the same. I ask her if she's got any spray for the mosquitoes. She explains about these green coils, you light them and they burn all night. 9:55 p.m.

9

I didn't even want the lettuce, I just wanted to chop it up and chop it up. It's supposed to be good for your skin, so I put some juice on my face. It's not a brain thing anyway, that's what I was thinking, massacring the lettuce, but I bloody well forgot it at the time. It's just not a brain thing and any enlightened person will tell you that. You can't engage on that level or you will never get it. I should go out and point this out to him but there's actually no point, because he's not interested in getting things. He only wants what he already knows. That's all he wants to get.

He's also sometimes gruff and he frightens me, his voice does, he's so full on when he's on, I feel like he's amphetamised or something. It's not the most prominent attitude, but it's there, a murky underbelly. He doesn't really even bother to camouflage it so it must be genetic—inherent. You can pass on karmic dispositions from a previous life; an angry dog woofing all around the joint.

I worry he's not predictable. Predictable people are boring until you're with somebody who's not. The lettuce chopping makes me anxious—I have this thought about sharp knives; Gary had huge knives for butchering, and I wonder whether I have the only sharp knife around or if there's another one and if there is . . . should I take this one to bed with me?

I decide to put the knife under my pillow just for the night. I can always put it back again in the morning. The thing is I don't really know who he is, normally I'd get an intuitive feeling and trust it. But I feel freaky and hesitant about my judgment now.

The water is running but I can't be sure, he could be anywhere. Shut up, shut up, shit—this is my head talking. Shut up, shithead. "Confetti," that's what Baba said. "Flotsam, pay no attention, flotsam . . . mind's always playing. Make clear lake." I can't, I try but I can't, my shoes keep popping up in my lake. I want them.

His room's bleak as mine, rough wood and plasterboard, pastel pink and blue. God, everything's hanging, pressed polo shirts, five the same in similar colours, two pressed jeans, blue and blue. I go to the dresser, he's got a whole nail kit, a shoe-shine kit, a sewing kit, Christ. They're all angled to the left, hope he hasn't got a penguin. Fuck, Kathy Bates was frightening, I can't remember whether she angled the penguin northeast or northwest, shit, she would have killed me. He's probably got some fanatical hair detection system going—hairs lined up across drawers. I'm in the drawer with the Grecian 2000 hair dye, half expecting Vaseline Intensive Care cream. No toilet bag, I like to look at people's toilet bags, see what drugs they're on. The shoes my mission. I check the far wardrobe, nothing, where are they? I feel around under the bed, it's dark. There aren't any, no bloody shoes anywhere. He must have taken his with him. Hell, he's too scary.

His stuff looks stiff and organised. I wish I had a sewing kit, it's so dinky, I feel like playing with it. Miniature cotton reels, with special folding scissors, a Velcro pocket full of buttons. He obviously saves them whenever he buys things. Tiny tape measure, bet he never uses it. I had a set of tiny chairs once, I loved them, I love miniature things.

God, I drop a cotton reel, it falls against my sari, I have to clamp my hand around it to stop it falling. Shit, he's out there, no he's not. He is—

He's in the fucking living room. Hell, I can't hear the water. He's inside, no he's not. He is, you idiot, he's calling out your name.

"Ruth, Rrruth!"

Shit. Jump out the window!

"Hello."

He comes through the door, his face tight, eyes scanning the room.

"Oh, hi."

"You're in my room."

"I know, I was looking at your sewing kit."

"What for?"

"It looked nice."

"Did you want something from it?"

"No, not really, it just looked nice."

"Uh-huh, humm . . . you want a shower?"

I did, I nodded.

"Yes, is it hot?"

"Yes, it was."

"Thanks."

Heh, heh, what a dope. I should have told him I was looking for my shoes. Now he thinks I'm a schizoid creep, pawing his private stuff. I can't really go back in and say I'm not like that, I don't normally do these things. Dummy—it makes me feel depressed and hot thinking about it.

The shower is hot, open to the sky, made of corrugated tin. I sit and meditate under it. I could have got away if I hadn't nosed around his stupid kits. His caring for things makes me feel I don't. Mine are plastic bags with bits. Damn! I could have had my period, no one thought to ask, blood pouring out of me, him heading for the hills. I should have said I was looking for a Tampax. That's what I should have said, I could have asked him to put one in . . .

I lie in bed listening for him. Not a peep. You'd think I could sleep, but I can't. I toss and turn and sweat, half think about masturbating but can't think of who— Whom?—to wank with. Half consider Baba, not really viable, disrespectful. Anyway it doesn't work, I can't get the fantasy going and can't wank without one. So I look at a nail hole in the wall, a perfectly symmetrical hole. Not big enough to put your finger into but deep enough to have no end.

"It's a black dot that will grow and fester and telescopically enlarge until it will consume you like a dark cave." That was my friend Zoey's answer to my "What's the point?" question.

She also said, "What's the point is not a question."

But at fifteen it was my question, I wanted to know what the point of going to school, of getting dressed, of living my life was.

On my wall next to the bed I drew a black dot and every day when I asked the question, I drew around this dot until it became as big as a fist and my mother noticed it.

"What's that black mark in your room?"

"What mark?"

I always asked a question while I figured out her mood.

"The saucer-sized ink stain, Ruth."

"Ohh that."

"Yes, what is it?"

"It's a despair chart."

"Oh why? You're not unhappy are you?"

"No."

"Well good."

Next week Mum took me clothes shopping and then we visited the wallpaper department at David Jones. She thought it might cheer me up to redecorate. I refused, I said I wanted my room left just the way it was. I was however happy about the new clothes. Mum confided in me that she finds shopping, personal shopping, good as therapy. While we were sipping milkshakes in McDonald's and Mum was sighing about dinner, I said, "Mum I'm fifteen, I want to know what the point of life is."

"The point, mmmmm, that's a very personal question."

"You mean it's rude?"

"No, it's not rude, of course it's not rude, well I . . ."

And she drifted off.

"I'll think about it," she said.

While we were waiting in line to leave the David Jones car park, she said, "It's a bit like a car, I don't know why it works, all I know is that it does work, you turn the key and the motor hums. You shift the gear stick to R and it goes back, to D and it goes forward."

She was looking sideways at me.

"You see, the point is you don't have to know, you just live, it works, you follow along. Probably there are some philosophers and experts who have studied the subject and know the ins and outs, but for us, it's not necessary, you can just go along . . . do you see?"

She looked at me again, smiling anxiously.

"The truth is," said Zoey, "there's no bloody point to our existence."

"God, it's amazing there is as much civil order considering we're all going to die anyway," I said.

"Yeah, like how come people don't just steal and rob and pursue pleasure as much as possible?"

"That's it, they aren't sure, worm fodder, it's too scary."

My black mark on the wall grew almost as large as my head. I thought I ought to do something to darkly celebrate, like putting a plastic bag on my head and tying it. But instead I sobbed for two days. It began because my hair had been cut two inches too short and I looked very bad, but that wasn't the real reason, the real reason was I hadn't discovered the reason to live . . . given that more people were mean and jealous and envious than were nice and generous and kind. Zoey thought I needed drugs, a distraction, so we took some E. I looked into her eyes and cried with joy. In Zoey's eyes I saw the solar system and I stroked her forehead and told her she was beautiful, that she was a person like me and our eyes glowed, hers were mine and mine were hers. That day I didn't feel lonely for the first time. I knew I was not alone on the planet, somebody had at last seen me . . . I worried about it being a drug induced discovery, but Zoey said, "Look, if it's all bullshit, if we aren't here for anything, let's just have fun getting through it."

I wake in semidarkness with chunks of wallpaper from my Sydney girl room floating about me. It takes ages for the hut to assert itself. There are dense silhouettes outside the window—still night.

I need water, I get up to get my sari, and pat along the chair, can't find it, no sari, not on the chair. Not on the bed either, or on the floor. Fuck! I go into the lounge, it's stupid looking in the lounge, saris can't walk. I tie a towel on and go out to the shower, no sari. I go back to my bedroom, check under the pillow and see the knife. The knife makes me sweat even more, the look of it—sort of beckoning. My hands are sweating buckets, I wipe them, they're still wet. I open his door, very, very, slowly; inside there's no breath, not a sound, he isn't even in there. Fuck—what the fuck is going on? I hate him. I drink and go outside, there's no one, so I pee out in the open. Behind me there's a bird noise, but no bird. The bird noise continues—I'm hearing wings flap, I'm standing in front of a tree with the wings flapping. I count off the branches up towards the whipping sound and am almost at the top when I see a plume of smoke hanging in the air. An extra long, long flag—my fucking sari's in the tree.

Ha, ha, ha, certifiable. The sari's too far up to climb to, I am not going up there for it. He's a prick, probably done this trick before, old dog teaches new tricks. Wroff, wroff. He's extinct, he's below extinction. I should have gone. . . . Mum would not have consented to this treatment, trying to lobotomise me, bullying me into admitting I'm not a spiritual person. Now I've weakened, he's on top, well he's not going to be. I'm not going to boo hoo hoo over this one. Over anything he has in store for me. I don't cry that much anyway, hardly ever. I tend to go, emotion coming, can't be fixed, move along.

The sari was a present from Rahi . . . incredibly soft cotton. It's the sort of cotton you want to bury your face in, it's so bloody gentle.

I look at the landscape, empty, just as it is, not fucking with my head, not like family. Go back inside to search for a substitute sari, no curtains to speak of, so I strip the sheet from my bed, hacking it up with the knife. Sit sipping tea with no appetite.

"Hello, who's that?"

"Guess, go on, who am I?"

"Yvonne."

"Yess! How did you know?"

"Well, Yvonne, it's not really that difficult, can I speak to Miriam?"

"She's asleep."

"Shit . . . Excuse me . . . Look . . . Yvonne, I'm in a hurry and I need you to do something, can you do something for me? . . . Yes, it is late. Can you come down here?"

"Have you cured her yet?"

"Yvonne, I can't talk now. I need you to bring some clothes down for Ruth—ordinary type clothes."

"Do you think dresses or pants? Dresses?"

"You decide, I'm sure it'll be perfect. Yes, it will."

I'm standing under a tree by the track, features are starting to define, no moon, stars still out. Southern Cross, belt of Orion, not sure, not sure, unfamiliar with Southern Skies. Could be Jupiter, Sirius! the dog star, the Pointers, truly amazing clarity of sky. I really do appreciate it. You don't see stars in New York. Damn. Where is she? 3:48, this is inept, irritating, my thoughts left pondering the sari.

Clothes or beyond clothes? Some exitors say it's a gimmick, an outmoded technique, like cutting off the Hare Krishna's ponytail, but often you *can* separate the cult identity simply by removing the uniform. It's a little simplistic, brutal even, but you have to put that up against the higher price of leaving someone to rot in an ashram. . . . Or so I soliloquise and get this worrisome image: me, meditating under a tree for two years.

It's 4:00 a.m. and I'm sweating. Shit, why didn't I pre-arrange this? Abandoning Ruth with minimal bonding, unprofessional—I'm starting to become them, that's why, one of the lesser endowed people. LOOK FORWARD, I do. I focus my eyes on the track. Of course she slides right past me. I yell out, "Yvonne!" just about killing myself. She reverses back in a foolhardy manner, straight snake all the way. But for Christsake don't compliment her, don't enter that crap, just dynamite fodder to that bunch, anything . . . any gap, and they're through it.

"Have you got the clothes?"

She has, plus she's wearing heels and minuscule shorts.

"Yes, yes and I've brought you coffee."

"I can't do coffee, Yvonne . . ."

"But . . . but, it's a gift . . . because . . . to contribute towards your meaningful efforts . . ."

Her eyes are welling up, tears poppin' out, mascara running. Jesus, I recant, thirsty anyhow.

"Okay, do it, Yvonne, do it."

4:20, 4:21, 4:24. Coffee is poured, handed to me, she flicks her hair back. One, two, it's very kind of curly.

"So, has Ruth been talking to you about her thoughts?"

"A little."

"Ohh," she's so lucky to have you. Someone to talk to. I have strange thoughts too you know." Her voice goes quiet, she steps up closer. "Robbie thinks I'm having an affair, he's found the letters."

"Uh-huh." I nod.

"Yes, Robbie's so mad he just wants to beat the guy up, but he'll never ever guess who it is." She sips at her coffee. "Shall I tell you?"

4:35. I nod. "Okay."

Her face colours up. "Me, it was me!! I wrote them. They were soo, so, beautiful and sooo romantic."

"Really?" I'm amazed. She is drop-dead gorgeous, I can't see why she'd have to invent this junk.

"Yes," she sighs. "I don't have sex with Robbie. I have sex with film stars. . . ."

I'm feeling agitated and pour more coffee. Her eyes shut. "Yes, yes." She says she cuts their pictures out of magazines and sticks them along the insides of her bedroom drawers, and when she's making love with Robbie she slides a drawer open and pretends she's with Keanu Reeves or Tom Cruise, whoever.

"In the dark I imagine Robbie's arms and legs are theirs. Sometimes I get a little confused, whose are whose, who is making love to me."

She drops her coffee cup, tormented. All of her is in the drawer.

I am listening, not expecting drama, and have to toss my coffee to support her.

"Hey, take it easy, take it easy, breathe into the diaphragm." I have to show her where it is, below the breasts, put my hands there. Get her pushing them away. "Yes, into the diaphragm."

My hands are being moved; we're massaging breasts now.

"Oh, thank you, yes, it's so important to get the breathing right, it's so hard to control it all. Do you have a web site?"

I ease my hands down with difficulty. "I've got to go." I get kissed, I kiss, the light is coming up.

"They took bets on you, you know."

"How's that?"

"The family. They bet on whether you'd win or not."

"And?"

"Miriam refused. She said Ruth would rather die."

11

He came in around six, in a froth. I had the venetians down, so he rushed straight past me into my room. No me, I relished that, it was like nectar—seeing him rushing 'round as he does now. God! it's exquisite. Oh, yes and he's seen me, sitting in my ripped-up sheet. Phew, yes phew, you . . .

He comes over, handing out clothes, none of them mine, two skirts of Mum's, floral tops and a purple top of Yvonne's with leggings. He's sorry he's late with the clothes, same here. He stuffs them back in a red plastic bag, shaking it at me. I knock the bag out of his hand. No reaction, he picks it up. He's too close to me, he's standing on my sheet. I try a surreptitious tug, hardly bearing his proximity—my hands wrench the sheet. He seems pretty flustered and jumps to one side. I say, "I had clothes or weren't they your choice, Mr. Coca-Cola?"

I say this very normal after hours of practice.

PJ springs to the kitchen, busies himself with a jug of water, like I obviously haven't spoken. He brings back lemons and glasses, glasses with ice, all very organised. The lemons are cut with my pillow knife, down and half, down and half. Apart from the large sweat blotch down his back, it's all very controlled.

"Drink?"

Oh this is stupid, this is so bloody stupid. No, I don't want your fucking drink. The drink is in my face, glass forward straight at me. Whack! I punch the glass away, it shoots up out of his hand, spills all over him, rolls over off the table and breaks up everywhere.

He smiles his difficult child smile, I don't help, won't budge. He stoops to pick up the pieces, methodically doing his job, his hand acting as suction pump, sucking up the splinters. Clearing one part then another.

"I want my sari back."

He goes and lifts the blinds, examines his hands, picking out glass and blowing on them before he speaks.

"You know, I thought I was going to have to wait the longest time to see the real you break through. You think a sari is going to change that? Ten hundred saris won't hide that. You'll only succeed in winding a large cocoon around yourself."

I shrug.

"This is crap. You're provoking me and then saying how dare I, how dare I complain, as if I should just sit here accepting your efforts to bring me down . . ."

"Are you down?"

". . . in your opinion."

"Are you down?"

"I said in your opinion. Look, what's the point of this, *are* you fucking down? Well I'm not fucking well up, am I? *Do not discuss the Lord with nonbelievers less their envy seek to kill your own.*"

He goes, "Ahhh, sorry who said that?"

"Baba."

He sweeps his hair back, mutters to himself, "Oh yes . . . very convenient, we couldn't have anybody questioning the illusion of you in the little sari . . . not so spiritual without it."

"You're unnecessarily rude to me."

That is it, I am not cooperating anymore, not with that sort of attack, he can do all the bloody work, that's what he's paid to do. I just don't want to sit here with him, that's the problem. I try and find a groove on the coffee table to escape through. I can't, there's not one satisfying enough. I need a really big deep groove.

Silence in the room. I haven't spoken, PJ's still inspecting the floor. He bends down and rescues a slither of glass near my foot. I pat my sheet feeling for flesh gaps. The parrots squawk in the tree outside. They squawk and squawk. I fantasise about walking down through a hole in the earth, a door that opens into a long spiral staircase leading down to a warm lake with a goddess on a throne in the centre. I desperately need to tell her what's going on so I don't bother with any formalities, just plonk myself on her lap, oh God sob, sob, I can't even speak, I'm too afraid I'll lie and she'll be bored. She is bored, sob, sob, we break apart in the water.

I'm looking at PJ, past him. My thoughts are still swimming with the goddess, sobbing and apologising. She's pointing to another me, over on the lakeside, irate, jumping up and down, tearing her hair out. "Don't worry about her," she says, "forget her," and puts her arms around me. I can't bear being locked up, maybe that's what lakeside me is screaming about. She's saying I should be screaming my head off.

PJ knocks on the table.

"Hello."

He gives a little wave.

"Could you share what you're thinking with me, please?"

He's relaxed, apart from humongous droplets of sweat. I can't even sit properly still without bits of me going—the hands, the feet, the legs, the nose, the hands, the head, the feet. I can't control a bloody thing. If I was properly evolved I wouldn't be prey to his opinion, I'd be beyond opinion. If Baba were here, I could ask him. I could say, when is a voice God's?

I speak, I say, "I was meditating on the essential difference between you and Baba."

I get given a glass of water.

"I know!" he says.

"Yes?"

"He wears a dress. Ha, ha, ha. HAA."

His face collapses with this funny. Christ: it's like old jokes about transvestites. Ha, ha, I say, very flat down inside myself. Ha ha ha.

"Actually no. He lives the way he teaches."

"He does, uh-huh"—still laughing—"and what specifically has he taught you?"

"To experience God. To want to be a good person."

I drink water.

"Uh-huh. How's this God manifesting itself? Are you out there doing good deeds and paying taxes?"

PJ's peeling an orange, all the peel is falling in a spiral. I tell him I'm in training. How I can't offer myself without self knowledge.

"Ruth, this is just about pissing me off."

Pause, the peel keeps going . . .

"What do you mean?"

"I've got the taste of bullshit in my mouth and I'm sick of it. That's what I mean."

"So who took the sari?"

He is staring in a totally different way, his eyes travelling through me. The orange dribbles down his wrists. He doesn't offer me any and doesn't look away either, still staring with the handkerchief out, wiping up the juice.

"The sari's a prop. As I said, I wanted to see what your spirituality was like and I saw it . . . peel without the orange."

I look at the spiral on the table, thinking of the peel's durability, but was warned against this type of argument in the ashram. This sort of Western-style argument being basically a barrier to the heart. Falling in love isn't logical, falling in love is essential to the understanding of the Guru.

He's probably violent, all those creepy mannerisms like peeling the peel off altogether and cutting the lemon in this precise way. I study his chunky meat hands, the way they break into everything, the orange, old sparky fingers, still fingering the handkerchief. Violent.

I say, "America's a violent place."

He squints at me. "Is it?"

"Yes, thirty thousand Americans kill each other every year; at least I don't go 'round murdering my neighbours."

"Uh-huh, yeah, and that's a very interesting piece of bullshit . . . what would Baba say? Did he teach you all about how good you were, how open and generous your heart is and how you can never be a bitch?"

This affects me, it sort of burns all around and through me—the pleasure of being caught.

I look at him, my mouth slightly open, smiling my little smile. He's smiling his little smile too. I drink—there's really nothing left in the glass, only drops, which looks dumb. I don't find that out till too late. He moves the water jug my way, which is really making me uncomfortable, as I have to decide: Do I pick the water up, admitting I didn't check the glass, or do I try and pour more water, which I'm not sure I can manage without bungling?

"You're a cynic."

Thump! He bangs his hands down, in a horrible scary way.

"Yes, yes, I'm a cynic, because I investigate crap. What about the crap in you, Ruth? Did you take that crap to the Guru?"

I'm looking at the table, looking at the table.

"You don't care about me, you don't even know me, and I didn't go to Baba to get my fucked-upness fixed."

"Well, you'd be the first."

I sort of nod.

"All right, so what, I hoped it would help me grow."

There's a pause, he nods, double nods.

"Uh-huh, good, Ruth. That's a start."

He pours me some water, which makes me feel pathetically weak—watching his hands work, wondering why mine won't. I feel I have to say something just to stop myself from completely disappearing, so I say, "Well, what do you believe in, then?"

And there's a pause, quite a long one, and he says, "Why would you want to know that?"

And I say, "I suppose I'm curious to know what you worked out."

And he says, "Why, so you can follow me? Sorry honey, that's not my ticket."

Said like I'm some kind of sheep baaing after him. Immediately my face flushes. That I'd opened to him made it awful. Really, really, awful. Like I'd exposed some doubt and he'd taken advantage with the putdown.

My face goes redder than a beetroot, I put my hands up to cover this and try to cool it down but it doesn't work, and he's saying, "It's all right, Ruth, just let it go."

I can't see things properly anymore. I take the beads that Baba gave me off my neck and finger them, concentrating just on them. I do this till I can stand, they're nice and round. Then I hold them out in front of me, and go running up and ram them in his face. I ram them in his face and run outside.

I want to hide. He comes out after me in shoes, so naturally he has the advantage. I turn abruptly into him and we collide, which sends him sprawling into me, he pulls my arm to save himself. I lose it, absolutely lose it. I would have lost it anyway but the touching does it.

"I told you not to touch me, I said, don't you ever touch me, my body is MINE! MINE! You're a prick. What's it feel like riding into town, sorting out the little woman?"

I turn my back and hop. He's there, I hear him, his feet, crunching at me. "Oh YES! this is so bloody good, I feel so bloody great."

He says, "You know, you'd be better off crying."

"Huh." I turn around and look at him and just bloody laugh, "God, that is so pathetic . . . it's what you want, isn't it?"

He shrugs, his hands are in his pockets. "No, but why not express the genuine feeling?"

"Fuck you." I walk on, he walks after me.

"I'm not interested in disempowering you. You can go right back to Mother India for that. See how they treat women there. Or didn't you notice all those little ultrasounds blipping away so's people can go in and say, 'Oh my God, it's a girl,' and flush her out."

I look at him, I didn't know. What am I supposed to do with that? I feel part of that female scrapheap, being female. Maybe they should kill us all, then there'd be no women left to shovel shit on. I kick at stones.

"Well, they're more honest." My toe stubs a large clod of earth.

"Sorry."

He doesn't get it, so I spell it out for him: "They're more honest in their HATRED of WOMEN."

"I don't hate women, I love ladies."

"Do you?" I say, just about nodding my head off. "You wouldn't know any, I bet you date dollies. Oooh, you so brainy, you so big. Me need expensive dinner to show 'ou off, after 'ou spend lots of money on me, maybe me suck 'ou off."

He's not impressed, his eyes roll back and forth. I walk away, sit down on a large flat rock. My head pulses.

"Can I be alone now? I want to be by myself."

He cautiously eyes the vast stony expanse.

"Well, where am I going to go?"

12

Ruth wants time out, I let her have it. It's afternoon, 2-ish. Day two, the twentieth of December. Could be Tuesday. I'm thinking about this, when she comes in, she wants to take her food outside—I let her do it. I don't let on but I'm grateful for the break. Ruth's still largely defensive, still scoring points. What's desperately important to her is dumb to me, no, dumber, to me. The pride, to be seen just so, handling it, all that seems irrelevant to me. Standing on a goddamned swamp and arguing minuscule amounts of knowledge you're bound to sink.

Fun. Are we having fun? I guess I am. She fights her little corner, hurls herself 'round, oblivious of everyone else. I take a lot of that because of the situation. She goes some bit extra—veering between vibrant, gamesie, aggressive/rudely aggressive. The vibrant's fun, the gamesie is the complicated part of the not so straight self. The aggressive is pure freakout, as in, do me a favour. The thing is you can't go getting angry with these mind control victims: she's psychologically trapped in her cell and she's going to kick the shit out of me for going anywhere near it.

The other thing is, women can wind and wind, no man will ever get a foothold on that territory. Too many dolls and chitchat interaction to no purpose. But this generation has the power, they can infiltrate, they don't have to small talk over coffee to no purpose, yet there still seems to be that innate windup built in. A genetic chip. Perhaps that's nature's compensation: they wind us up, we can't stand it, we give them power.

Didn't enjoy her attack on misogyny, my inferred misogyny. More, I was hurt, thinking her quite attractive at the time. That she doesn't exactly swoon at the sight of me is my protection. But to be thought repulsive is another matter, to have her recoiling her arm with obvious revulsion is nasty. Not that I think I'm magnetic, well maybe I do, mentally I do. I don't think I'm physically disgusting either.

So, when she didn't dig you, you didn't dig her, did you? Yessssss. Thank you very much, I'll note it. Keep the personal feelings out, label job hazard and don't fall in.

As regards the business at hand, the sari point worked, true spirits don't fold, and she folded. I was equally pleased with the text over trust lesson, though unconvinced she has in any sense woken from her "I experienced it, therefore it must be true," position.

Most people feel similarly, they don't question the experiential process, they're starving for the release, the love—whatever their emptiness dictates. They don't want to think it could be manipulated, conjured, projected. The thing is, it works—manipulation.

I've seen a girlfriend of mine combust in a fit of crying she was so overwhelmed by the touch of a Holy woman. She hadn't seen this Holy woman before and didn't believe in anything specific enough to call religion. She lined up in the queue, which stretched for hours, leaving her standing in the hot sun. During that time she witnessed/heard several sobbing exhibitions as she stood there. Finally she arrives in front of the Holy woman and she shrivels, all her verbal preparations dry. She feels naked, she doesn't know what to do, she realises there is no way of acting, no procedure. The Holy woman does nothing, says nothing, her eyes steadily engage with my friend's, who willingly strips herself of herself, shedding all the blocked pieces of character she's been hiding for years; deception, jealousy, anger, all fall into the Holy woman's lap, they heavily embrace, she experiences complete catharsis and sobs into the Holy woman.

My friend said later she felt this woman knew her and accepted all her wounds, she understood her and why all the hurt had existed, and that this acknowledgement was deeply healing to her. I also acknowledge the unsaid appendix, which is that Joyce lost her mother at the age of six. The Holy woman caught that loss.

Ruth is studiously contemplating stones, gathering a whole bunch of medium-sized white stones. I startle her on my way out to the john, she immediately pulls her sheet around. Squawk, one of those mangy crows greets me from the toilet, I sit and throw paper pellets at it, peck, peck, no fear, hops and pecks. I'm not going to intrude on Ruth for a while, see if she comes back in to have a peck at me.

There's a sponge cake in the fridge, it looks home-baked, I want to scarf the lot, better slice it, you never know, she may want a piece, especially if I've assumed she doesn't. Hummm real eggs, golden, real jam, mmm, I love jam and cream. No women bake these days, mine doesn't, she says if she did I'd expect it. Really? She's right, I would. She says it's better if we both earn money which I appreciate having been with women who don't. Their brains go and they don't accept the slave role, which is basically the position of a dependent. Carol says that's ancient talk, but admits she expects staff under her to do as they're told.

It takes strength, but I return a quarter section of sponge fantastic to the fridge. A tomato rolls out, which makes me look at the floor, which unfortunately could do with a sweep, a mop even. I do both and feel good, cleaning always does that for me—the more you do the more you can do.

Cults usually offer discipline, all Krishna communities follow a more or less similar timetable:

3:30 a.m. Rise and shower
4:15-4:30 Morning deity worship (*Mangala-aratrika*)
5:00 Chant *japa* (*Krishna mantra*)
7:30 Scripture reading and lecture (Also time for chanting of additional rounds)

8:30 Breakfast. End of morning devotions
9:00–12:00 Various work schedules
12:00 p.m. Noon meal (*Prasadam*)
1.:00–3:00 Various work and rest schedules
4:15 Afternoon deity worship
5:30 Shower, dinner, and free time
7:00 Evening class at temple
8:00 Retire for sleep.

Same with the Moonies, four to five hours sleep, robotic schedule, out all hours selling trinkets on the streets, never alone, loved up on all sides: "You're wonderful, dynamic, nice, good, smart." Same could be said of the armed forces with some crucial differences; there is no omnipotent leader, it's not a closed order, the mind control such as exists does not require recruits to mentally block against all other points of view. I know, I got organised in the Marines.

I peek out at Ruth again. She's hunched over her bunch of stones, clicking them around conscientiously, some sort of rockery—that's the appearance, which is positive. They could do with a few tame shrubs.

We have a wee ways to go, Ruth and I. I figure we're less than halfway through the cave. Sometime soon she'll know she's lost and will start looking for me to lead her out.

3:05 p.m. I make tea. The sky's so blue it looks wrong to me, must be the absence of pollution. Everything's intense, red earth, silvery grasses, animals out of the ark. It's so damn big. I like that, I like that about America too. . . . I should ring Carol, not sure of the time difference, something weird like fourteen hours, shit, five in the morning, she'll freak. Better rein in Ruth instead, see if she'll gravitate of her own volition.

I go out with the tea, herself not having made much of an effort in my direction, vacuum cleaner dynamics, sucks out what she wants and moves away. She sees me, I don't move, sit drinking my tea. She clops on over, takes her tea, manages a "thank you" and clumps off again. I go inside, she follows.

The hut's pleasantly warm. We sit in our prescribed positions no one's actually designated, she sprawled or cross-legged on the green couch, me feet on the floor in the armchair, which could be old red leather or maroon, I'm no good on reds. Not colour blind exactly but the subtleties elude me.

"Aren't you supposed to ask me questions?" she says.

"If you want me to," I say, without facial expression.

"Why not?"

"You partially want me to?"

"Yes."

"Okay. Was taking your beauty off to an ashram the ultimate revenge?"

Long, deep sigh, probable suspicion. She has her

thumb and forefingers pressed against her head, her elbow rests on the other arm. Sigh.

"Beauty has its own price, you wouldn't know."

I look, her face has gone deadpan like mine. "Attracts the shit?"

"It can do."

I wipe my hands.

"I've dated some beautiful women in my time, models. My ex-wife was a model. A bit paranoid, she was always obsessing about fat people. She looked good though."

"Oh right."

"Excuse me?"

"She looked good though."

"I'm not with you."

"Very sad."

"Is it? Well I might be being a bit dim here but I don't understand the innuendo."

Deep sigh, quizzical look. The two fingers supporting her head twist a section of hair around.

"It's your attitude, you're saying she looked good so that excuses her stuff about fat people."

"It doesn't excuse her stuff about fat people, it's simply what she said."

"You said, 'She looked good though.'"

"Yes she did. Aren't you ever critical?"

Pause.

"Not about fat people."

"Have you ever been in a dishonest relationship?"

I get a nod.

"Then you'll know how painful it is."

I feel muddied in her eyes after that, the beauty exchange. Interesting how she was waiting with her foot out ready for me to fall. Cough, she clears her throat and swings her head around, fingers alive with tea cups on the table. I pour more tea, Ruth pours milk and crosses her legs, helps herself to a sandwich, all food still transported via the right hand. I decide this is the moment to personalise myself, introduce myself as story.

I could begin anywhere really and feel half-nauseated with the boredom of being adult fodder. But Ruth doesn't need the intimate details, Adam and Eve in the condo. So, on from fat people.

"Yes well, that relationship wasn't that fantastic, as a matter of fact, there was a kind of hostility between us. She, my wife, Toni, would often feel vengeful, avoiding discussions, in fact they would panic her and make her feel worse. That would lead from one no-go area to another no-go area. Till there were so many cumulative no-go areas we could hardly speak. That led to her suggesting open marriage, which we did, went to key parties, did some pretty weird things—mostly her initiative. I screwed around, she screwed around, her father died and left some money, so we went to India. Disastrous, there were six of us on the bus. Her putting on airs, getting very flirty with the friends, next thing I know, she's

off having sex with my best friend, Tom. So I punched
him out and left the bus."

Peripheral vision tells me Ruth's sliding her foot
along the ground. She brushes some grit off her foot and
tucks it in beside her. Violent postcards zip in my head;
the fury I felt for Tom at the time. The woman trying to
sell peanuts by the roadside, my foot pinning his neck to
the ground. My fist thumping into it. His hands fighting
to protect his face. My fists thumping into it. Peanut
woman touching peanut child's bare ass. Blood everywhere.

"I wanted to die."

"Why?"

"Because I had nothing: no friends, no wife, I was
completely alone. No one needed me. That's when I met
Singh. In Goa, he lived on a mini-Disney site out of Goa.
Had its own street lighting, canteen, hospital, school,
prayer hall. It was hot when I arrived and they gave me
pepper water and rice to eat. I became a toilet." No reaction—Ruth's flicking hair across her mouth.

"Anyway . . . we all, all of us American disciples,
stuck together and drooled this putrid competitive
chatter around Singh. We'd sit and swap best boy
stories: the special hug, the Divine IQ test, the fake
phenomenal world, the trinket I'd gotten or she'd
gotten. Singh loved us more than a hundred thousand
Western mothers, Western parents, very, very, selfish.
Grandparents split apart, no duty—*The ego must realise*

its unreality; the individual soul is a shadow. So that was my mental state, *high,* God-intoxicated. You want the truth, you believe it's him. I did."

I go to the fridge. My throat's dry, despite the tea. We share the water, Ruth pours! I glug it down and continue.

"My surrender came the day he visited us on the porch, which was where us Americans slept. There were four others mooching about with me, but he walked right past them and straight to me. He talked very quietly and everything else fell away as if I'd been transported and he was channelling a heavenly state. We embraced, he left. Don't know how long this went on for, felt like minutes, probably seconds. Can't remember a thing he said, shook all night, and in the morning I was his. Did anything he wanted; typed up his translations, led prayer meetings, nothing was too much for me. If crap happened, I put it down to test, Singh's testing me. All was bliss. Then one historic day he took me to his private rooms and hugged me. I thought, I'm special, he's chosen me, very happy. Next thing my fly's unzipped, my tool is out, my dick's hanging in his hand and he's rubbing away."

There's hush in the room, Ruth is staring; for the first time she's physically still.

"What did you do?"

"I'll tell you in a minute."

I take a drink and wipe my hands.

"So? What did you do?"

I'm telling her, when a low droning noise interrupts me. We both look to the ceiling where the engine noise is very loud, a plane. She hears it, obviously. We see it swooping past the window.

"What's it doing?"

"I don't know."

"Well, is there an airstrip around here?"

"I don't know, it must be spraying."

She doesn't know, all she wants to know is what I did with Singh.

"What I did with Singh was pack and leave the ashram, in what transpired to be a pretty threatening scenario. I'd been there two years, a most dependable slave. So unfortunately, he's waiting, standing some- where out there en route. I slip out the back way along dirt thoroughfares. There's nobody about, I start to wonder if they've shut the gates and can't see till the last building. The main gate is shut, the side gate's open, so I walk as fast as I can towards it. There's a few people I know who scuttle off when they see me, I'm calling to them and patting Mangy-dog when Singh steps out in front of me. He's all in red, looking at me, and I have to walk past him. As I approach he begins to growl, this very low growl like a beast, 'Urrugh, Urrugh.' With every step it's a little louder, 'Urrugh. Urrugh,' till finally, as I draw parallel, it's so goddamned loud my chest vibrates—and he hisses at me: *'You show only outer love, inner love not complete, only delusion.'"*

Voorummmm. The plane's back, my ears follow it—she speaks:

"God, what did he mean?"

"It means, well . . . to me it means, uh-oh, I didn't come, he couldn't fuck me."

Ruth is processing this, fingers circling on top of her glass.

"You don't think he could have loved you?"

"Ruth, I thought he was God."

"Oh."

She comprehends this—chews it over. Her eyes follow the plane overhead.

"Yeah, I guess that is bad."

BBrrrING!

The cellphone rings unexpectedly, we jump. I take it outside. It's Miriam, she sounds breathless, shaken.

"How are you, how's Ruth?"

"She's listening, she's at a delicate stage."

"Oh good, did you hear the plane?"

"Yes I did."

"Oh good, because. . . . Hahh it's terrible. Hahh. We've had a call from air traffic control, a pilot rang them."

"Uh-huh, what for?"

"They . . . hahh . . . they wanted to know if we'd left a help sign down near the hut."

"A what!"

"A help sign made of stones."

". . . are they going to pay us a visit?"

"No, I said it was a game, I didn't know what else to say."

Shit, what to do? I run to where Ruth was arranging the rocks. There's definitely some pattern to them, must be quite effective from above, white stones against this reddy-coloured background. I'm standing in the loop of an incomplete "P." "P" for protest. This is bad, how did I not see this? I didn't, I was totally taken in. Revenge of the sari . . . should have expected some comeback gesture and didn't. Obviously the three days' contract interprets liberally for her. I'm going to call her out, one thing no one expects these days is consequence.

I go back into the hut, very, very slow, very slowly, my eyes adjusting to the light. There she is lying on the floor, back towards me. Her hands are holding up some photograph. Legs relaxed, waving at the knee. I watch as she presses the photograph to her lips and kisses it. I steal up, watching. Waiting . . . near her head I stop.

"What would a Guru do with a disobedient devotee?"

She's kissing a photograph of Baba's feet, hardly aware I'm there. Her lazy voice says, "I don't know."

"Oh, so does he say, shucks wah boo, I won't have it, or does he turn a blind eye?"

She rolls over on her right side, right hand still fiddling with the photograph.

"He would throw devotees out if they continuously disobeyed him."

"And do you think that's fair?"

She thinks and says, "Yes. Yes I do."

"Good," I say, and bend my knees and pick her up as best I can. She giggles at first, thinks it is funny, then it isn't funny, and she bashes away. I get her by the hands and drag her out, she tries a bite, it doesn't connect. Then she accuses me of touching her, touching her body. Obviously all touch is sexual to her. I throw her in among the letters.

"You're dishonest," I say.

Her retort is, "You want to sleep with me."

13

He does. He threw me on to the ground, really roughly, saying you're dishonest, "You're dishonest!" Shaking his bloody finger at me—*you, you*—all because I wouldn't break for him. And the touch was sexual—how many times do you ordinarily need to touch a person? You don't, this pisses me off with guys. I'm sitting there, grazes up my arm, my knee's scraped and I'm shouting, "No you! You're the fucking hypocrite. You're touching me because I won't break apart for you like all those other chicken-wing girlies."

Snap, snap, I sort of imitate the bones snapping with my hands—cracking them apart in a loony frenzy. I knew he wanted to sleep with me, so I said so. He stared at me, his eyes hard, not saying anything. It was a cold look, I looked away . . . the straggly trees, the hills, everything seemed cold, fearful, as if he'd managed to make them that way—all part of his pathetic attempt at justification. Which went on and on, and then he came, stood right over me, and said this really bitchy thing, he said, "Not all touch is desire. But you"—forefinger pointing at me—"you wouldn't know about that, would you, Ruth, because you're so busy up there"—forefinger tapping skull—"imagining how everyone is desiring you. You're one of the most ungenerous people I've ever met. I don't think you could actually entwine with another person on account of your having to put out."

I fell for that. I shouldn't have, he doesn't know me.

"We made a contract, Ruth, which you broke."

So what! Of course I'm going to try and break free, shit—I'm bloody kidnapped, aren't I? Something he wants to ignore. And, in any case, I don't have to honour a contract with the devil. Hee, hee, hee. I told him that, which got a big reaction. He went nuts, halfway towards the hut, he stopped dead in his tracks. I got scared thinking he was going to hit me, couldn't move and started counting *1, 2, 3, 4, 5, 6, 7, 8* in my head. Still counting as he marched over, virtually into me—*11, 12, 13, 14 . . .*

"I'm a regular person an' you know it. Now put those stones back please!"

Shit, I don't know why he's so mad, he started it—if he hadn't bitched in first, the devil wouldn't have come into it. But he hurt me, it was on a personal level, nothing to do with religion. I put the stones back, which annoyed me. I did it because I didn't want him to think me a totally rigid person, "unable to entwine." Stupid to bring up the devil in that position—when I was on top. Stupid, stupid, to give him that, that card, only fed him more. And anyway, I have had deep relationships.

I was piling up the stones, thinking *lesson learnt; you create your own reality*. Although Baba said this was a problem in the West, the self God, something about the self being an endless mirror of deceptions. I tried to remember what he'd said about the wholeness of us all, some concept of indivisibility, which was incredibly interesting and instantly left my brain.

I'm worried Mr. Pressed Jeans is trying to get me to swallow his version of reality without checking it. Worse, I realise that the sum total of my collective, educative knowledge is utterly slack, a regurgitation of facts. Essays written with no actual thought required. I'm really beginning to wonder if I'd know a choice, having eaten all this crap—I've never bothered to question stuff I instinctively felt was right.

He's probably created this confusion in my head so he can sleep with me. Overstating my perceived selfishness in order to break and fuck me. Part of me thinks, *This is true, he's right, I am greedy, uncompromising,* whatever, and another part says, *Why do you even care what he thinks?* It's the kind of attack all visionaries have to put up with, the constant battering to test insecurities because the bloody testers just can't stand the possibility it might be true. How can I protect myself?

I go back into the hut and eat the single piece of cake allotted to me. What a guts, stress eater, he doesn't seem a typical gutser, he seems in control, unlike me. He's washed the dishes again, guilt, guilt, another assault on my personality. He's sitting relaxed, waiting for me, what am I supposed to do? Sit with him? He's making me feel responsible, as if I should be indebted to him for being here.

I have a headache, I don't want to beg for a pill but I'll have to. My feet look dirty too, God I'm a wreck.

"Have you got headache tablets?"

Yes, he has aspirins, he must use them to thin his blood. I take three. There doesn't seem much point in talking. I'm looking into PJ's eyes, they're hazel, he smiles, I say, "I've got to go to sleep."

"Well you can."

"What do you mean?"

"I mean I'm not stopping you, sleep if you want. They'll be collecting us at seven-thirty."

"Who?"

"Your family, Tim, Miriam, Yvonne. We're going up to the farmhouse, we're all going to watch a tape together."

"What sort?"

"You'll see."

"*I Left My Brain in India?*"

He takes this seriously, almost applauds me. Destroy, destroy, just because things went sour for him, at least he wears deodorant.

I go to shower, asking *if I may* for Christsake. In the bedroom I catch sight of myself in the mirror on the inside wardrobe door. A ghost. I go up and inspect my sheet, it shows more flesh than I thought, but that's not what alarms me. I don't know what it is, the absence of any personality in the room or my ghost face. And even though it's hot in the room, I feel cold . . . it's something in my head, some idea. I'm wondering, how do you know for sure if someone loves you? How can you know it's real . . . even though I felt those feelings, were they what the other person felt? What matters more? That Baba doesn't care about me, doesn't love me? Or that my love wasn't appreciated, wasn't felt . . . Or, or, that the love itself was an illusion, completely worthless. I shut the door.

The sheet/ghost outfit is out. Banished. It's a choice of Mum's elasticated batik skirts, her floral tops, or Yvonne's ultra purple top and/or leggings. I choose the skirt and feel like an exhibit, a thing, a doll's house woman plonked down in the parlour. That's okay, I can be their doll, lock my fears inside my little wooden body.

After the shower I find PJ pacing about in the sitting room, he's changed to look smart. Clean, but identical jeans, yellow sports shirt, and cowboy boots. Poor thing, he's really trying, smiling and doing everything possible not to make crooning noises over my skirt. Sure he wants to . . . probably wants to get down and kiss the hem.

Shit, I don't want to go!—exhibit meets spectators. I sort of fidget and feel sick, very nervous. He brings me water, I take it and don't sit down. I'm so bloody agitated I have to walk. *Ohh* God!

"Can we not go up to the farmhouse . . . please?"

"No."

Oh, fuck, how predictable. He's enjoying this. Why? Why do I have to go through this mindless spectacle—I kick the couch.

"Then I'm angry, because I live in a democracy without anything democratic happening to me."

His tongue bulges round his lower lip. "Can you be straight without the grandstanding and tell me what it is you fear?"

This is it, I can't. I don't want him getting down on me.

"No."

"Okay, that's fine."

Yawn. I pull some hair around my nose and sniff it. He's wiping at his face again.

"What time are they coming?"

"I told you, seven-thirty."

"So what's the time now?"

"Twenty to."

Shit! I may as well sit down, don't want to go into the bedroom, don't want to be anywhere by myself. I kick my leg, watch my ankle circling 'round and 'round. We sit in silence and more silence. I want to leave the room—finally I blurt out, "I want to know how other people behave."

He shrugs his shoulders, "Like they are."

Yeah . . . I look at him and look at the floor, what's the point? Deep sigh.

"No. I want to know how they behave with you in this conversation."

"I'll tell you, if you'll tell me how this will help you."

I chomp my bottom lip. How would this help me . . . it would help me to see how to behave according to this situation.

"It'll just help me."

"Okay. There are exceptions but generally people tend to behave over the three-day period pretty much the same as they would in the outside world. Applying exactly the same strategies and attitudes they apply in life."

He's right, that doesn't help me. I suddenly want to cry but don't because I don't see the point in that either.

He gives me the penetrative eye treatment, I brush at my top, making sure my breasts are not on display. Pat, pat. He's just staring, feet apart, torso forward. It's bright outside and dark in the hut.

"Can't we talk outside?"

"Too distracting."

"It's dark in here."

"Turn on the light."

I get up and stroll across, feeling his eyes on me. My hand goes up nearly missing the switch, I'm so preoccupied with the graceful execution. Why didn't he turn it on, instead of making me feel conspicuous, performing for him?

There are two lights: one above the sink, the other above the chat area. All they do is light the top of his head.

I saunter back, careful not to trip, which I wouldn't do if I wasn't being watched. I sit, picking up a glass of water.

"How well do you know yourself, Ruth?"

Heh, heh, my glass hand shakes and is wobbled to the table.

"Don't judge it, speak it," he tells me.

"I want to."

"Well get on with it."

He laughs. "Ha, ha, ha."

I say, "I don't know myself perfectly."

This produces more hahs and thigh slapping. He asks me how I feel I've behaved.

I yawn but don't feel disinterested. "You tell me."

He leans back, his face has a *forget it* look.

Oh all right, what's it matter? "Angry and suspicious."

"Excessively suspicious."

"Oh, fuck off."

"You swear too much."

"I swear."

"You do. Too much. What brings on the suspicion? Is it a natural resistance or did something specific happen to you?"

I don't really understand him so I say, "I'm not sure, I guess I look for a particular weakness."

He points a finger and says, "Uh-huh, in others?"

"Not only."

"Good," he says. "Can't change other people's landscapes."

I think about this, a big doll's house with my large hand moving things about. I'd like that. I could pick him up and drop him on top of a tree, force him to obey me. My fingers pulling down his pants and beating him with matchsticks. He could cry and cry and I could pass him tissues.

"Did Baba have any faults?"

Groan, I don't care, I'm in my doll's house fantasy.

"Yeah. He was enlightened so he must have been a con."

"Humm," he goes, lips smacking, the obvious irony landing, splat, down the banana shirt.

I say, "Sorry," for no particular reason.

He says, "Why? You're right, they're cons. They con themselves. Being a holy man's a better life than being exploited in some factory. So why not, why wouldn't you construct a whole new identity? Chidaatma Baba relinquishing himself from a life of broken limbs—an inspired option."

"What is?"

"The role of holy man, constructing yourself as a holy man."

"Hold on. Shut up. I don't think it's that easy—who'd believe you for fucksake?"

"You would. You'd self-hypnotise, persuade yourself of your vocation, visit real holy men and woman, study them, study texts and in time, after the first devotees have fallen for you, you'd believe. You'd start demanding surrender and people would do it, people love surrendering their souls. Wow, no more me, wow, what a relief, she can do all the carrying. I'll just sit here, over here, and meditate under this nice little tree."

"Hooray!" I stamp my feet and put my bum in the air. PJ simulates an up-chuck, pushing fingers down his throat, clenching throat, hands together catching the pretend up-chuck. Pretend up-chuck is then thrown to me. The spoiler. Me, who lets it fall, splat, which gets interpreted as allowing my responsibility to fall. Which is in a nutshell, the role of devotees. I don't believe him, where's the proof? His face is, well, not ugly, firm, set in some resolve. Oh God, I didn't say I didn't believe him, I just don't care. Christ, he's stomping off to his room.

Rustle, rustle, rustle.

A black plastic folder is brought back in, *Chidaatma Baba* typed in a clear plastic slip at the bottom. Inside are the before and after photos of a fifteen-year-old girl, thirteen when the incident took place. The before photo shows a girl in Indian dress, thick white-blonde hair, holding a microphone—a cutie pie, sensational eyelashes, extra-blue eyes. The after has her in leather shirt, piercings everywhere. Stud in her lip, cheek with chain to ear. The rape occurred when she was thirteen, staying at the ashram with her parents. She describes the special room Baba's bodyguard took her to: pink, with a small gold Ganesh in the middle, she remembered because she wanted one. (Actually have seen this door, but not gone through—too old, tee hee.)

Blah, blah, blah blah . . . she was told to lie down and that Baba had chosen her. She was given a robe, which he procceded to undo, oiling her breasts, stomach, pubic area. Penetrating her with his fingers and penis; when she shouted out, he forced his fingers into her mouth. All was suppressed till Baba asked for further favours. Susan eventually broke down and told her parents, who complained. They were told they had "wrong understanding" and left disgusted. Were followed and harassed by phone calls requiring eventual legal intervention.

I plonk the folder on my chest, PJ's over by the fridge in body only, washing glasses, his mind's with mine. He takes down a no noise cup, I strain back up into Susan's photograph, each end of her mouth curls gently to exactly the same point. My finger whirls around each curl, sweet, sweet, eyes, I wonder if she had to blow him, poor baby, I want to hug her.

I turn the page loudly for his benefit, he hears, same sort of stuff. Monster Baba puts in penis, intimidates devotees. With a little footnote about a French boy who died eating blessed Baba dust instead of antibiotics, he had a simple urinary infection. Another page, fifth generation farm—donated . . . page starts to go blurry.

My head is collapsing, I rest the book across my face. In my experience the normal world's where everything's covered up; at least in the ashram, people were open about their lust. A couple of guys got angry with me because they wanted to have sex with me and thought I wouldn't be interested, so they'd get mad and say, "I'm angry because I'm ugly and I want to have sex with you."

It was almost a turn-on, the biggest turn-on for me is honesty. I think I could fuck a weasel if he just said, "Okay, I'm a weasel, and even though I'm a weasel and not even of your own species, I want you to fuck me."

I could love him for that.

14

Honk, honk, the clowns are coming, reference her brothers. How do I know? Because of the noise they're making, intermittent horn blasts from beyond. Pathetic, each honk jarring the countryside. Miraculously, Ruth doesn't wake. Minutes of peace left, and due to (for the umpteenth time, I want to shout, scream) *lack of backup,* my concentration meanders. I keep doing mental countdowns, we're up to: Your trust is beautiful, so are you but don't misplace it, the results are disastrous. I'll run through various cults, well I will do, that's the video. So far all I've given her is the Chidaatma dossier: she thought she knew him, *I know him better*—that's what I should have called it, or *Evil the same everywhere,* or interrogative, *Is evil the same everywhere?* You'd probably have to, have to stipulate, you can never damn well assume anything. Some people say there's no such thing as evil, it's merely a concept designed to irradiate descent. I say, "Yeah, interesting, until you meet it."

Thank God she's not wearing that fucked-up sheet, not abandoned for the right reasons, of course, no renunciation or anything, but abandoned nevertheless. Sending a meaningful message to the family: success (we hope). And I do hold the key, I knew I'd find it, you don't need vivisection, you need complete attention. Smooth the person out, make them feel comfortable, then you need to lend your whole self, all your powers of observation to that subject. Who if nothing else feels the flattery of that attention, allowing them to drop theirs. Stroll around, play with elephants, help, not help; exposing the usual patterns of behaviour. Particularly visible if you minimise sleep, with that additional deprivation all sorts of inhibitions fall away, defences weaken, risk-taking becomes easier, that's the brochure. Not so clever having mine equally deprived, but I'm getting clues, more intense and accurate than the staggered cross-referencing I'd have built up with a partner.

The key to Ruth, for me, was personal development. Ruth has a healthy self-interest, almost as if she wants to get whacked and explore her own inner world, *inner,* note: too bad about the outer, interpersonal relationships, but she's got the feelers out. Ashrams don't focus on individual fuck-up, there's little behavioural challenge, people can go in and out complete pricks but very religious. So I hold the key to that, plus the old adage 'No one but a fool wants to be caught worshipping one.'

However, with Ruth so attacking, I haven't been able to flatter her in the usual ways. We tend to mooch off into other areas, areas I'm not so sure are relevant, but keep her present, so to speak. Conversations like how other people behave in sessions, interesting to her, boring horseshit as far as I'm concerned. Although how she in particular behaves in sessions, her pathology, does interest me. It offers a faintly luminous alternative to the usual donkey work I do.

But—and this is the big one—it's not within the prescribed exit counselling dynamic. We're getting into behaviour perilously close to the psychotherapeutic, which is and is not my job. It's fine explaining how a cult works and her allurement to it, not so benign excavating her own inner workings.

The dilemma for me is I'm tired, and the psychobabble gives me access. It's easier going down that route—why a personality like hers, superficially on top, should find itself within a cult. It's not totally unorthodox—we do look at family and social impact, but her behaviour shouldn't be the emphasis. Cult, cult mechanisms, how they rob individuality and individual potential, i.e., we focus on the immediate crisis. That doesn't mean we never experiment, and this could be the time.

I steal a look at Ruth, snoring under the hard evidence. The black book keeps me out of her face, she has a great face, very mobile, all kinds of weather on it. Her body's open. I feel duty bound to peer at her breasts, so I move closer and sit and stare at them. If she hadn't gone on, their intrigue would have been incidental. They look very soft. . . . Actually all I'm seeing is her chest moving up and down underneath dense material and imagining how my hands might feel fondling them, and thinking . . .

Honk! HONK! Slam!

The nuts are here. At least with them around, I can concentrate on my *own* performance. I had to have the whole damned tape converted to PAL, global economy don't make me puke. I do feel some tension over this goddamn video demonstration. It's the aloneness and fatigue, and the thought of it, *too,* seizing up and ineffectual, is something I couldn't easily countenance at this stage of the proceedings. I don't have the bravado, whatever, to deal with terminal failure. I've never allowed it to happen before, could be interesting to watch the bricks crumbling apart in front of me, but I think with this particular family someone has to maintain vigilance—me.

Tim walks in and wakes her with a kiss, a precise set of actions; book removal, perspiration wipe, kiss. She's so tired her lashes are crusted with sleep, we have to feed her coffee. I get a hot washcloth, she pats it on her face. Robbie helps himself to the fridge, I don't even react, no one speaks much. I ask if the video's working? It is. They've checked it? Yes, they've checked it. Tim comments on the clean floor, he stands in the middle surveying the room, slowly turning—feral.

We go outside, the sun is setting, we drive with it, heat and emus and everything jumping have a calming effect. Soothing. The sun is huge, a golden pumpkin orb. Ruth's sitting next to me in the back, I smile, she smiles back falsely bright, her knuckles are white on the side of the jeep.

An emu with tinsel on it rushes by—madhouse coming up. Wholesome hot food, I hope.

"Are we having any food?"

"Nope, I've eaten it. Couldn't control myself."

"Good for you, Robbie. So is there any?"

"Yeah, of course, can't hold Puss back. So, do you know about tacos, taco food?"

"In what respect?"

"Taco chain respect, franchises."

"I'm really here for your sister, Robbie."

"Yeah I know, how's it going?"

"It's going."

He lights two cigarettes and passes one to Tim.

"Sweet. So are taco bars still doing well in the US? Taco, Taco Bell . . . I've heard you can make a bomb from them."

Tim punches Robbie on the arm.

"Quit the tacos, you senseless moron. No one wants to hear about take-aways."

"I want to know."

"You would! Everyone else is into organically grown, pesticide-free, non-genticised . . . Ouch!"

A punch from Robbie swerves us off the track. Punch, punch, horsebite, punch, we thud over a rock, Ruth's head judders on the back seat. Tim resumes bickering.

"Fuck you."

"Fuck yourself, you bastard, you always get what you want. I can have a little talk with him, can't I?"

We are travelling through pink, unspoilt, enormously vivid landscape, tremendous rock formations with strangely gnarled trees. And this putrid, you can't even call it dialogue's going on.

". . . I'm just trying to get on for Christsake, if you wanted a bloody franchise, you'd pursue it."

"All right, Jesus. Please tell him about the tacos. I don't want to be responsible for his missing the big opportunity."

"You have to be collateralized."

"Is that it?"

"Pretty much, they're very expensive."

End of tacos. 8:04 p.m.

I want a drink so badly I almost genuflect to the farmhouse's ugly television aerial. Sprinklers, cut lawns, flowers, it all spells civilisation. Yvonne's out front, wearing a shiny, tight pink dress, not a speck of dust on her, all smiles and kisses opening doors for me. I get the dainty hand treatment, squeeze, squeeze. . . .

"Oh my goodness, you must be tired."

She whisks me off into the living room, Bill Bill jigs his glass in the air—can he get me one?

"Scotch on the rocks, please."

I note the decorations, I can't help but . . . The

place has been transformed into a full-blown Santa's grotto; fake snow, glittered window frames, and fairy lights on the picture rails. Everyone stands as I enter, Toddy rushes up to show me his broken arm, all covered with cartoon stickers. Bill Bill taps on it, I get my drink.

"Where's Ruth?"

"Behind you."

"Oh darling, you look wonderful," said uncertainly by Miriam, who goes to kiss her on both cheeks. Ruth pulls away.

"Doesn't she, Gilbert, she looks wonderful?"

"Yes, you look good, Ruthie, can I get you a drink, what's the poison?"

"Gin." Ruth crosses her arms and walks head down towards Robbie.

"We can do it with ice, can't we, Bill Bill. Do you want ice, Ruthie?"

There's an attractive corner near Yani, *Tim's boyfriend*, which is how I'm introduced. Early thirties, ethnic origins, voluptuous features, nipple rings visible under the T-shirt, thick hedge of hair covered in goo. His arms flop around Puss, whose hair he's just dyed. She shows me the intricacies of hair tint, parting her hair this way and that.

"He's got such a sensitivity for it, see, it's marvellous the way he's threaded all the colour through. You tend to go one way, till someone shows you differently."

Yani comes over and squints at mine, he tells me to vary it—jerk!

The television's been placed on boxes draped with furry sausage garlands and a horrible plastic fairy holding nasturtiums. Fat chance of a serious message. I look around for Ruth, who's having a drink poured for her by the moral imbecile, read triple whatever, Robbie. And another straight alcohol for Yvonne. He gets himself a large tankard of rum and Coke, whiskeys for Bill Bill, Gilbert, Yani, "Mummsie," Tim, and Puss.

I look around for Fabio, "Fabio? Still with us?"

"Nope. He had to work poor bastard."

"Ohh, that's a pity." (Said enigmatically.)

I tap loudly on top of the television and ask for Toddy to be removed, a hushed fuss breaks out between Robbie and Yvonne. They leave to squabble in the kitchen. An assortment of chairs have been arranged in two semicircles; some don't fit together well and have to be swapped, more time ticks by. Puss sits up front with her crochet, Gilbert and Bill Bill arrange their feet on a "stumpy." Miriam pulls in a table for her whiskey, Yani and Tim bring in what looks like a bong, but isn't, it's a melted beer bottle ashtray with silver indents. They share a chair, which is, well—Homo.

Yvonne returns and sits up front next to me, Robbie sulks in the kitchen doorway, only one thing's missing— Ruth. She's at the fridge helping herself to Bill Bill's ice machine. Clink, clink, clink, we wait, the thing goes on forever, clink, clink, she walks across the room, eyes into the carpet, very, very, slowly. Then there's an age (literally minutes) while she tries out chairs, makes decisions; one has a cushion, the other has arms. The cushion's transported turtle speed to the armchair, no it's no good. She prefers the armchair without the cushion, it's transported back again. Painful.

I begin.

"Fanatics have their dreams, wherewith they weave
A paradise for a sect, the savage too
From forth the loftiest fashion of his sleep
Guesses at Heaven; pity these have not
Traced upon vellum or wild Indian leaf
The shadows of melodious utterance.
But bare of laurel they live, dream, and die;
For Poesy alone can tell her dreams,
With the fine spell of words alone can save
Imagination from the sable charm
And dumb enchantment."

A bit of a hush has entered the room, thanks to Keats, which shouldn't be impressive but is, because so few people can memorise these days. Yvonne claps, Ruth's indeterminable. The cigarettes come out, in a clicking frenzy.

"What was that?"

"Keats."

"Oh yes, Keats," says Miriam. "I love Keats, *Ode to a Nightingale*:

'Darkling I listen; and, for many a time

I have been half in love with easeful Death.'"

Robbie (from door frame): "Axminster carpets."

Me: "Yes?"

"They quoted Keats."

Me: "Yes?"

Tim: "They appropriated Keats: 'Beauty is truth, truth beauty.'"

Miriam: "Oh yes, that ad went on forever."

Tim, Puss, Miriam: "'. . . that is all Ye know on earth, and all ye need to know . . .' Marvellous, wonderful, he died so young."

Me: "Uh-huh . . . Yes I know the quote and you're right. That's exactly what they did, it's exactly what cults do. They appropriate language, strip it out, reload it to suit themselves, thus we have the dumb enchantment. Yes?"

They get it.

I focus on a light above their heads, a red fairy light and restart the mind control hypothesis, which reminds me of hypnosis, which triggered the Keats poem that alludes neatly, *normally,* to language loading: "Language loading short circuits the brain's response. Can you all stand an example?" Yes they can. Because I'm not stupid enough to wait for an answer.

"Maya. A lot of Eastern cults play with the word 'Maya,' claiming our world is a coarse illusion in which we're all playing parts. The real world lives behind this veil. Now, just to confuse you further, this is a legitimate Hindu belief—but Western people, some of us, tend to swallow this non-real world very literally. They then, some of these people, tend to go on ad infinitum, labelling all previous existence as coarse and irrelevant. If you're a Hare Krishna, for example, there's a temptation to bracket all life as *Krishna's arrangement*. Whatever happens to you is explained in this way. Basically it's an attempt to simplify complex issues that either threaten or confuse people."

I point to my glass. "Anyone like a refill?"

"No thank you, no thanks," is the response.

"The thing is I don't want interruptions as I go, so I'm suggesting that *now* is maybe the time."

There's a lull, nothing happens.

"So you're all sure about the drinks?"

"Yes," "No," "Later . . ."

"Good, because mind control can be a pretty tough subject and I don't want people scrabbling around for drinks. . . ."

"No, we're fine."

"Might help you relax." I press.

"Wait!"

At last Bill Bill gets up and walks to the drinks trolley, we all watch. He's touching the gin bottle, vodka, steps back, goes for the whiskey. Up behind him go Miriam, Puss, Yani.

I wink at the others.

"Heh heh, you others get the point, yes? The drip, drip, factor? Subliminal advertising—crummy products, drinks, you really need one . . . good. All right everybody, let's sit down again."

"What?"

"He said, *sit down*."

"What about the drinks?"

"You didn't want the drinks; he made you think you did."

"Why?"

"It's how they work in cults."

"The term *brainwashing* translates literally from the Chinese *hsi nao* as 'wash brain.' First described by the American journalist Edward Hunter, who was told of its use by Chinese informants following the Communist takeover. The process came to be known in the West during the Korean War when a considerable number of captured Americans appeared to have swapped allegiances, many believing they had committed fictional crimes against the Chinese."

Tim and Yani find this funny. When I ask why, they blow me kisses.

Ruth's chair is empty, I insert the video.

Thousands upon thousands of brides in white dresses stand at attention with their suited husbands in an austere concrete stadium. Footage of a mass Moonie wedding in progress; as they bow with sombre faces we cut to the tops of trees, sweeping slowly over the jungles of Guyana, dissolving through into documentary footage of the Jonestown mass suicide. Bodies bloated and strewn over planked walkways, higgledy-piggledy, all over each other, on through rough huts and up to a chrome and vinyl throne.

Finally we have shut down—the reality of swollen bodies in the sun. I see Ruth standing by the door, part lit by Jonestown, Miriam passing food to Ruth, she takes something, I don't see what, she feeds this something to the cat. No, SHEEP, for christsake. The goddamned thing's got a red fluorescent stripe down the middle of its back.

"On the 18th of November 1978, Congressman Ryan and three journalists were gunned down at an airstrip near Jonestown, Guyana. At five-thirty that day, Reverend Jones spoke his last words: 'If we can't live in peace, then let us die in peace . . . Take the potion as they did in Ancient Greece. This is a revolutionary act.' Shortly after, nine hundred thirteen members of the cult known as the People's Temple, including two hundred sixty children, drank a Kool-Aid mixture laced with cyanide. Mothers began feeding it to their babies through syringes . . . Those who showed a lack of enthusiasm were shot. Many of these children were wards of the State of California adopted by the People's Temple to provide income and serve as unpaid workers."

Yvonne's hand is on my knee, pinching, she doesn't want to see a baby sacrifice. I tell her there aren't any, she bats her eyes, breathy and warm. I lean over, removing her hand, her leg presses against mine. The fucking sheep drops its fat ass in front of the television. Where is Ruth? I twist to see, she's sitting back in her chair, legs crossed, head in hands.

A young woman in her thirties fades up, she sits like a newscaster, dressed in a seventies-style polyester suit and tells her story straight to the camera.

"When you meet the friendliest people you have ever known, who introduce you to the most loving people you've ever encountered, and you find the leader to be the most inspired, compassionate, and understanding person you have ever met. And the cause something you never dared hope could be accomplished and if all this sounds too good to be true it probably is. Don't give up your ambitions to follow a rainbow."

Interval. Robbie pours me a whiskey, Gilbert grabs it, adding extra ice and soda. Puss hands me three chicken rolls, a Christmas napkin, and a thumbs up. Miriam rubs my arm, she likes the show.

"Oh yes, so moving. That young woman, what happened to her?"

"She was murdered, driven off the highway by unknown assassins."

"God." She shakes her head. "Don't tease me, John."

"Would I do that?"

"Ha, ha," she laughs. "Hmmmm."

Tim and Yani raise their hands, I ignore them, they continue:

"What about school?"

"Yeah, what about parents?"

Boring. "Social conditioning's a fact of life. We're not debating normal social requirements, we're discussing destructive"—they shout me down—"cults." . . .

"MY FATHER, my father said to me, he said—'No boy of mine's growing up straight.'"

"Shut up you."

"He used to put me in dresses, Yani, it was so cruel."

"Haaa. Hah hah hhhaaaa." Puss totally explodes.

Yvonne wants to know about transcendental meditation, about cosmic channelling and UFOs. I look at Ruth who stares back with an unsettling intensity. She stares past me to her mother, focuses on her, then off her and onto her father, then Bill Bill, Puss, Yvonne, Yani—it's not an engaging look.

15

I could see everything and I was calm. Every little detail, Yani's nipple ring, Bill Bill's pale towelling shirt, the hair on his legs, the hair on Dad's. Dad's bony feet, big toe shorter than the next. Mum's neck, two stray hairs caught on the back of her blouse. The low ceiling, the yellow chairs with flat arms. Yvonne's drink, Yvonne's cigarette, and him. PJ. He was removing her hand from his thigh, placing it back in her lap. That's when I knew what I'd do. It wasn't clearly formed, but it was there, a vague revolving idea, giving me hope.

Whenever I moved, PJ reacted like his skin was psychic. I would move and he'd turn, seeing me. I had to keep shifting because I was zonked out and nodding off. That and feeling uncomfortable, hated for causing all this. Like, for example, Robbie ignoring me in the doorway, just about managing to pour me a drink, poured without speaking. Mum and Puss so careful of the fucked-up Ruth, who would have died in Jonestown had she been there, who would have armed herself heavily and shot at police, blown apart for her crazy beliefs. How crazy of her. I didn't know what to do with myself, I was wandering about arranging bits of food, not really able to concentrate, every now and then I'd catch something from the telly, feed the sheep, and stroke the cat and start replaying Susan's story, the girl from the Black Book, inside my head. Her sweet, sweet, eyes. She was lying back on Baba's bed, his hands massaging in circles down her stomach and into her vagina. I blinked it away.

The family seemed removed. Distant aliens with lots of oral habits, chat, chat, chomp, chomp, smoking and drinking. They stomped up and down as well—no idea really; which I quite liked. I hadn't done as a child, I'd wanted efficient parents with nail kits. Yani and Tim were the only ones who touched with affection, everyone else bumped. The cults seemed organised in comparison. Slight exaggeration. I wasn't exactly impressed by David Koresh. His place looked shoddy, old chicken huts in the middle of a muddy gray paddock, big deal—enormously threatening. The might of the FBI called in to incinerate . . . that sort of pissed me off, the intolerance, down-and-outs shat on, they weren't getting anywhere anyway, he was a bloody gas pump attendant who ran a band that no one listened to, who played crap tunes like "God Rocks." Which could have been funny but probably weren't. God Rocks, la, la, in your socks, la, blah, God Rocks, hump, hump, through your jocks.

I see Puss looking for a reaction, I smile weakly and drink. They'd all be so happy if I joined the oblivion. Puss's cat sucks at my fingers, she used to suck ear lobes and wake them in the night, so they introduced fingers. I pull my fingers back to concentrate on the brainwashed Chinese girl; her eyebrows crease together, forming squiggles—an extra pair of eyebrows on her forehead. She said she and her friends had loved Western classical music, but the communists thought it was unhealthy and she was forced to go to meetings to discuss this. "They said, French composers like Debussy give the people queer thoughts and funny ideas. That if we listen to Debussy we will feel as though we are under water or watching the sea. They say that since there is really nothing like this, we will begin to think abnormally. They liked songs that named all of the historical figures— like Mao. They said that these songs enabled people to get educated with a healthy spirit. . . . I couldn't find a solution. . . . I thought maybe their music was healthy, but it was not inspired."

Her voice is sounding off into monotone, and I'm watching thinking, Why on earth did she bother even considering their argument? What could a bunch of musically untrained soldiers possibly know about Debussy . . . Makes me mad on her behalf, and think, Why didn't she just pretend to agree with them, and like, Why not lie? The family is totally engrossed, fag smoke rising, can't even hear a plate scrape. Grace is looking more and more entombed, now her friends are changing their minds, trying to give her helpful advice:

" . . . They told me that when they believed in Western music, they were merely looking at life from the narrow standpoint of their own personal enjoyment."

"I was very confused . . . I felt lonely . . . I kept thinking am I asking or wanting too much for myself, and is this what makes me feel so bad? . . . When I was young I always expected too much—so now I expect the worst."

Horrible, especially the *wanting*. No one speaks, they don't have to, Grace Wu has invaded and spoken volumes. Grace had expected too much, Ruth also expects too much; selfish expectations end in brainwashed turmoil. The family basks in agreement, they were right, thank God we kidnapped her, can you imagine the burnings, plagues, and *sex* he might have had with her. Erugh, unbearable! Their frantic interest causes me to squeal inside, I want to go out but know this will be scrutinised and read as, "Cracked—she's cracked." It takes me minutes to stand up, I honestly think they'll do something, rise and chase me with hatchets. At the door I whisper, "Toilet," to Robbie, who lets me rush past him into the kitchen. I bang through the fly screen door and walk to the outside toilet past the frangipani, whose heavenly scent comforts me. I break some flowers off and sit smelling them on the loo.

There is something bothering me about Chidaatma Baba. . . . If the feelings I had in India were real why can't I sustain them? He said he would always be with me and that mind was a condition, not a place or person. But I can't love an abstract. I don't have the magic tricks PJ has. And anyway, why hasn't Baba rung me, he has my phone number, he could have rung me up in Sydney but he didn't. This thought really, really, enters me—and this is what PJ has done. You could destabilise anyone. You could sell love and say it was love and not have meant it. I've never thought of playing with love like that, but PJ has shown me how. Someone is outside the door, guess who? I can't tell, it's too dark, all I can see are the toes with long toenails. I go, wah, waah, sob for their benefit, they leave. I put my finger in my mouth and trace "Mental torment" along the toilet wall in spit.

Back in telly cult world the show is over, everyone's smiling at me. The spy outside must have spread my wah waahs, there's concerned flummox.

"What can we get you to drink, Ruthie???"

"Water, please."

"Of course my love," says Puss. Cluck, cluck, to the fridge.

". . . and my makeup."

Mum's eyes light up. "Ooh. Where is it darling?"

"It's in Tim's car, somewhere. Small, see-through plastic case."

"Robbie!"

Robbie jumps up, dragging Yvonne with him, who doesn't want to go.

PJ stares at me, I stare back, it's the first time I take full control of my eyes, we blink out simultaneously. He walks round collecting plates, building stacks of them in the kitchen. He starts to rinse, and keeps working until they're all cleared and everyone's helping. I get the ashtrays, I hate cigarette smoke anyway, if I blew anything up it would be a fag factory. Mum's impressed, me helping, PJ so humble and so intelligent.

She pulls me into the hall, we stand apart, her eyes are anxious, she wants to know how I am *really*. I look at her but don't know what to say. If I said, No, no, it's not all right, what would she do?

"Oh well," she says, pulling at her fingers, "it'll get better, just look at you now."

No one knows what to say. The dialogue we have is trivial anyway, apart from *doing*, what we're all up to, there isn't anything. I don't know how it happened, we love each other, but we don't communicate, maybe we did once but I can't remember.

Mum embraces me in tremulous arms.

I say, "It's all right, Mum, don't worry about me."

The journey back is silent, headlights and stars. I get Tim to turn on the radio, some old warbler sings something I've never heard before:

So long Marianne, it's time that we began,
to laugh and cry and cry and laugh about it all again.

Tim asks me if I'm cold, I'm not, no one is, it's hot, I shake my head . . . busy with my plan. Yani jollys us along with stories of his atheist parents whose favourite quote was O'Hare's interpretation of the Lord's prayer: "An utterance muttered by traumatised paranoid worms grovelling for a meagre existence." Tim laughs. They tore down Santa, the Easter Bunny, and every other fairy Yani was ever interested in. His father even paid a store Santa to tell Yani he was wearing a costume. Tim laughs.

We get to the hut. Tim and Yani leave. They don't say anything. Tim pats my arm.

It's dark, neither of us has left a light on. Again I had expected him to, and again get depressed wondering why I didn't do this simple thing. I hardly remember how I got out of the building, which worries me. There's a sort of blankness in which I'm wandering about, uninvolved. He's sapping my energy. If you tie someone up they just rot. Fuck, I'm so furious about this situation, watching him turn on more lights. It's really pissing me off. I run up and plant myself in front of the nearest switch.

"I can turn it on myself."

"I know that, Ruth."

"Yes, but you're assuming things, you're acting as if you're the only person here who can do anything."

He walks around.

"Is that how you're feeling?"

"Huh? Oh God, what are you on about, you just want me to say something, just say what it is and stop pissing me about."

He says, "All right calm down."

I say, "No. Don't you try that!"

He gets cross and says, "What? What are you on about?"

He knows what I'm on about, the superior shit is what I'm on about, so I tell him, "Just be honest and say what you mean, John."

"Well that's good, Ruth, I do, Ruth."

"You do, do you? Yes, by the way thanks, I loved the show, it was incredible, all those stupid believers, how could they do it, we're all the bloody same. Let's just get on with it."

He takes out his handkerchief, goes over to the sink and pours water on it. Comes back dripping, wiping his face and hands. "Thank you. Thank you for telling me, I know how hard that was. I respect your feelings."

Then he gets up and goes to bed, without even checking me, that's it! He's bloody gone.

I try to lie down, but am too tense with vengeful thoughts of myself as lunatic hirer, hiring a gang of brutal thugs to tie and bash up PJ Waters. It's so satisfying to see him open the door, struggling in surprise as he's lifted up, overwhelmed, and strapped to the couch. I sit with a cup of tea in a taffeta dress, watching their belts undo and flick across his bum; 1, 2, 3, 4 . . . 5. YES! YES! The crazy shit is I can't leave him alone, I have this craving to go on and on talking and saying things. Anything I want, being anything. Bad, terrible, I don't care.

In the dark, I meditate; my mind's so full of chatter it doesn't stop. I plan my plan. My plan starts with a banging door, at 3:00 a.m. I will bang the outside door. Just after three I will stand naked outside the hut, swinging the door back and forth, counting in my head, swish, swish.

Bang and Bang! it bounces back again. The sari flaps above me, curling in the wind, it looks like—fire!

One more time and BANG!! it's really loud, he must wake up. Oh my God he has, lights come on. I dash behind the tree. He calls out my name, his shadow passes the window. "Ruth?"

The sari looks fantastic. Flaming, spark of bloody genius, lighting up the sky. His mouth is hanging, gaping at the tree. He goes towards my hiding place but it doesn't matter, he can't see me. His eyes are on the blazing sari.

"Ruth, Ruth??" A hunk of sari breaks off and floats above the tree.

He's screaming my name.

"RRRUUTH! RRUTH!"

In a quiet voice I say, "I'm here."

"Ough. Shit Ruth, you frightened me." He staggers 'round. "Oh, Oh." He's very nervous.

"Hey, they were funny weren't they?"

"Who?"

"Those believers." I fold my arms and laugh.

"People do evil things Ruth. Where are your clothes?"

"In the wardrobe. It's not cold is it?"

He starts to pull off his shirt.

"Oww—my head's sick. My head is sick. Please, pleeaase hold it," I groan and moan.

I stretch my arms to him, he tentatively holds my face, tears running over his thumbs.

"You're doing well, Ruth, you truly are."

"Nobody likes me."

"They do, they care."

"You don't like me."

"Yes I do, I do."

"Kiss me then."

"Listen, I like you, but I can't do that."

"I'm freaking out."

"I know, but me kissing you won't help. Let's just cool, huh, go inside."

I walk forward and kiss his chin, his neck, his hand pulls up between us, separating me, I take his hand to the middle of my chest and place it on my breast, my eyes beg at his.

I ask him if my body's offensive.

He shakes his head, "No Ruth, no, your body's not offensive. You need clothes."

My arms are touching his, "I don't, I need you."

He shuts his eyes and turns away. "No."

He keeps on walking towards the hut. If he walks through that door it's finished. It's all over. I scream, "Stop! Stop!" thinking, I will have you, I will! Then when I'm just about on him I let it go, it's loud, he stops in shock. I'm shocked too; that I can do it, have pee running down my legs. I give him a long full kiss, tongue deep inside. He's gasping, mouth panting at me.

"We should ring your mother. . . ."

No one moves, we kiss again.

"Okay," I say, "let's ring Mum."

In bed his skin is rough. He wants to carry on kissing, I don't want to, I want to nail him and close my eyes. His penis is in my hand. There's a shaft you're supposed to rub, I never know where or if I'm doing it right, till they complain. He kneels right up by my bum, stroking and arranging my legs. In my plan it was me, my arrangement, but he can't handle that so I lie and let him position my arms and legs. He's a pump man, in, in, in, which suits my temperament. I don't moan much, which you'd think he'd notice. But no, he's pleased, all he wants is in; I can't stand it, I move my feet over his shoulders and tell him to go in.

16

"What if I hurt you?" I ask.

"You won't," she tells me. "Do it, just go in, go in."

I do, I can't help myself. I almost shoot immediately. Her pussy feels so perfect. I stop still. I want to make her happy, so I close my eyes and take my hands from her breasts—touching them's too difficult. I pin her wrists, which shakes her a bit, I feel her shift so I move with her and in her. I kiss her hard, she deserves a hard fuck, she beats at my back with her heels. I go deep, deep as I can, part punishing, part loving in rhythm with my thrusts, hard soft, hard soft. When she says, "Don't come," well Christ do I come, my whole body comes, everything is in my dick.

Next thing I'm lying back drifting when the bed wobbles. Ruth is rubbing herself through the sheet, I reach over and push her hand away, "Hey, I can do it."

"You don't know how I like it."

Her hand travels back, I slide mine over hers: "I might get lucky."

She humps this information, I suck my fingers and reach down. I know what a clitoris is and what to do with it, two minutes in she adjusts my fingers. I let her, I want what she wants. I'd like to know what she wants. She comes, using my fingers as a dildo. I want to reach out and reassure her, instead she sidles away, burying herself in the sheet.

I wake late to the sound of a distant car. My foot touches Ruth, I shut my eyes again. Mmmm—whose room are we in? Mine. . . Shit, what am I doing? You're sleeping with Ruth . . .

FUUCK. Jesus! Get up, I do, I have to, heave myself into jeans. My hands stink of sex, I run and turn on taps and squirt dishwashing liquid onto them, wash my face in dishwashing liquid. Run and roll deodorant under my armpits, throw on a T-shirt, sniff again, sniff, panic, rush into Ruth's room, grab her possessions, re-arrange them in mine, put mine into hers, can't wake her—additional chaos. They didn't go into any of the bedrooms anyway, they're not going to know the goddamned difference. Clean teeth, drink water, meet them at the door.

"This hut is out of bounds."

Tim tries to peer in over my shoulder. "Is she okay?"

"She's sleeping."

"Right."

Yvonne approaches with a plastic-covered tray of croissants. She nudges Tim. "Go in."

"He doesn't want us to."

Yvonne gasps. "Oh, but we're not strangers." The tray digs at my chest, she's going to get on in. "Do you mind?"

Yes, yes, I damn well do. . . .

She bustles past, naturally Tim follows her, why did I bother?

"Great. Why don't you . . ."

"Oh silly," says Yvonne. "Stop being strict with us." She wags a finger as she butters the croissants. Tim eats one, I chomp my way through another.

"Gosh, it's a mess."

"Thanks Yvonne, I washed the floor."

"Hmmm, did you? Hmmm. Where is she?"

When I tell them Ruth's asleep, they both go, "Oh."

Tim wants to know if she's accepted they're all crap?

My eyes squint at him—he looks away, he often looks away.

"You understand there are genuine religions?"

Yes, yes, he does, he means cults.

"You understand there's a difference?"

Yes, yes, he knows. "So how's Sis feeling?"

"A bit tender." A muscle twitches in my cheek.

He nurses this information while Yvonne pours the tea. She passes me a cup, I clutch it, it's boiling hot, I pull my hand away and get her to put it on the bench.

Tim takes his and drinks it, borderline machismo. He tells me Yani's sister's coming up tonight, they want to take Ruth out. "You know, celebrate. Get out."

"NO."

"What?"

"No way, she can't leave here, she's far too vulnerable."

"Why?"

"Because, you have to, you have to complete the. . . . the—what? What is it?" Yvonne's eyes have popped and frozen out behind me. Shit—Ruth. I bet she's naked. I spin round to see a towel-clad Ruth propped up against the bedroom door.

"Well I want to go," she says. "I think it would be good for me."

We all gape as she waves at Tim, ignores me, returning to the bedroom.

Tim shrugs. "It'll be a bit of fun."

Yvonne taps my arm. "Ruth has to have something to look forward to or she'll go back to India. Everyone needs to relax, all the health experts say stress is a killer. People don't realise how serious stress is, endorphins are important. People are important, not jobs, jobs don't give birth to you." She looks at me:

"You need moisturiser. Do you use a face soap?"

"No."

"Well you should, Tim does, don't you, Timmy."

"Yes."

Big wink, collects tray. "Goodbye, Goodbye."

I go back in and wash with water. Ruth is going out and there's nothing I can do. I have no authority, I slept with her, she could have said something but she didn't—she protected me. We'll have to talk, I'll apologise and . . .

and, and, and, I sip the tea. It's not impossible, we have all day . . . .

In twenty-three years of professional counselling I haven't slept with a single client. Not never, ever, but not while actively working. I've slept with some of them after. Only four, five counting Carol, who's still technically my old lady, if that makes any difference. Oh, fuck, forget it! I don't, in my heart of hearts, regret it.

Knock, knock. No answer.

"Ruth."

"What?"

"Can I come in?"

"No."

"Well, I'm sorry, we have to talk."

I go in, the window's open, she's dressing, sitting on the bed. There's a comb in front of her, the predominant feeling is she's young, which kind of brings the situation home. I sit carefully apart from her on the bed, the extreme opposite diagonal. Her face is very concentrated, which makes me want to sleep with her again.

"I'm sorry, Ruth, that should never have happened. I . . . I don't know how it did, because frankly it hasn't happened before."

She laughs at me, big wide laugh. It did sound dumb.

"All right. All right. Of course it's happened, but never in this situation."

The comb strokes the bed, big pause.

"Don't worry, it wasn't anything."

She combs her hair, strokes it down towards her face, the sun catches particles of lint, dust threads floating in the air. The sheets are stained, which is painful, in light of what's been said, the light making them so damned obvious. I find myself fiddling with different words, saving the nasties.

"Look I was there too, you know, it was a little more than that. I was trying to be comforting."

"That's nice?"

No look up, she can see me, but I can't see in behind the hair, can't tell what the true upset might be.

"I enjoyed it myself."

She giggles, shaking her head in disbelief.

"You were tricked," she says. "I tricked you."

This is delivered, head up, forefinger pressing into her chest. I, I, I.

I'm looking, thinking, okay then. It's not what you want but I'm going to obey you. I'm taking a shower and I'm pretending like you. No rescue, nothing, you can worship yourself. We can call it—she can call it whatever she damn well pleases, she's the client, all phantasmagoria are open to her. I'll call it, what? A minor setback? A diversion away from her more major obsession, the worshipping of qualities outside herself, supposedly located in quasi gurus.

She takes all afternoon to prepare, long shower, hair drying in the sun, makeup. Then she borrows my scissors to cut down a pair of leggings; I snooze, probe lizards in the blazing sun. It's peaceful, teeming with wildlife, all sorts of incidentals you wouldn't notice, large insects, flying dragonflies, probably snakes—I haven't seen one (I am one.) Then there's the odd steer as well as emus, and a winding dried-up riverbed where the stones have worn quite flat. They're warm, almost hot, stone pancakes. I spend time searching out the best to take home as a memento.

We would have been, in normal circumstances approaching stage 4. *Oh please! My guru is not to be compared with those nuts, Jones, Koresh, Rajneesh etc. Oh no, please he's not.* . . . Second wind for client, I empathise, but hammer it hard. He is, but it's okay, you aren't a fool in this. Your faith is beautiful, it's just he's not. Argument now (possibly permanently) on hold.

Trouble is I'm not so beautiful either. 6:45. We sit with our sandwiches, she's making tea. I try to do two things, look at her and rid myself of guilt. The guilt will stop me being effective and she was in on it as much as I. So as soon as that evaporates I can continue; in the meanwhile it's downtime. The incident seems to have cheered her up . . . which makes me wonder if anyone can help her.

"More tea?"

"Thank you."

"Are you coming to the pub tonight?"

"Only if you're going."

She hands back the cup—not quite—it's placed in front of me to avoid accidental touch. I should have actually said it then, said: If I'd refused to let you go, would you have told them? . . . Will you tell?

7:55 p.m. They arrive. We're ready. Yani is wearing Saran Wrap with a zipper. Repulsive. He introduces his sister Meryl. Composed is understating it; hot night, her hand is dry, token tinsel round her wrist. Face slightly flushed with sun, otherwise pale. Black bob, black dress, black heels, tall, well-worked-out body with bad manners.

"Hello, I've heard a lot about you."

"Good I hope?"

"I don't know, I don't listen to other people's opinions. Shall we go? I'll go with Ruth."

"Then I'll go with you."

We head off in two Christmas-decorated cars, read: vulgar shimmery gaudy sausage stuff, plus moose head, "Rudolph," fragile (amateur) papier-mâché trash wired to Robbie's fender. That's the theme: Christmas, "We do it every year." Robbie and Yvonne drive the Ford Falcon, the rest of us asphyxiate in Tim's Mazda. Meryl pulls at Ruth's hair.

"You lost weight in India didn't you? Everybody does. I'd love to go there, is it any good? I thought I'd do a yoga course, somewhere attractive—is there anywhere attractive?" Ruth's face twists away from her.

"Oh sorry darling, sorry. We won't discuss it, upsetting isn't it." Withering glare at me. "Humm, upsetting. That lipstick's too pale on you. I've got some Versace, bought it in London, didn't think they'd sell it over here, of course they don't. Pink-purple, you notice it. Most lipsticks are too boring, I don't know why people buy them. You've got nice lips, Ruth, you ought to push them out a bit, you don't need collagen—pain like you wouldn't believe. Open up, I'll do it with a brush."

Meryl's flicking cylinders, makeup purse, brush. I can't see, she's purposely turned her body from me—one leg on the floor, the other bent up at an angle near Ruth.

There's nothing on the interstate (being in the middle of nowhere and Australia), so Tim swerves out abruptly, drawing parallel with Robbie. Yvonne mouths out, "Hi." Robbie circles his hand 'round indicating slow. He holds up a massive joint, lights it and giggling all the while he sucks on it greedily, in out, in out, the cars nudging ever closer. Meryl tumbles into Ruth. "For christsake, grow up!" Robbie leans right out the window, his chest across the middle divide—white line wiggling underneath. Yani starts to climb out through the sunroof, he kneels up, pelvis full in my face. Please. His head cracks violently back—surprise, surprise. Howling hurricane

necessitates safe transfer—back to window. Yvonne
steers Falcon back to Mazda, Yani's hand meets Robbie's.
They pass the joint, peel off. I watch the joint pass from
Tim to Yani to Meryl, who helps Ruth, holding it against
Ruth's lips. Ruth passes it to me, I take it and throw it
out the window.

We park, and wait for Meryl, still labouring intently over
Ruth. Licking eyebrows, fingering lips. Again I say nothing and ask myself why all this irritates so much. The
physicality seems petty, not reason enough, but it is! I
feel proprietorial towards Ruth: she's mine, she's my
client, my responsibility. The others are mellow,
stretched out and smoking cigarettes. Yvonne hauls me
off down a side street full of low-rise, large plot homes,
verandas supported by thick brick pillars. Plastic swimming pools, flowers, dogs, cars, and massive omnipresent
aerials. Yvonne casually laughing. I feel impatient, want
to bust the aerials apart. The street leads to a Civic
Square, with gardens, monuments, and night life.

I catch Ruth whispering to Meryl, "I'm so hot,
I'm sweating, my whole body's sweating." So kiss-ass
provocative, I repeat it in my mind: *"Sweat, sweating."*

Outside the bar I'm approached with dope by a fat
boy, lopsided ears, fleshy lips, he's selling ready-rolled
buds, I shake my head.

"Fourth generation blonde?"

"Not interested."

"It's cheap . . ."

"Not interested."

We move through, swallowed by a group of heavily tattooed individuals, cowboys (well, cow hats) with missing body parts . . . several fingers and one arm, obvious enough to comment on. I ask Yvonne, who asks a local, who explicates the perils of farm machinery, arms gesticulating wildly: Would she like a drink?

I'm dragged on in, eyeballing a bar full of brassieres, hundreds of them hanging there, limp, grimy soft furnishings, Grade A turn-off. Through to the dance floor, where purple floors meet purple tiles travelling halfway up the walls. We sit, it's a Victorian building, ornate mouldings, and mirrors all decked out in fake cotton snow. Strings of blimping lights compete in odd, fast, slow rhythms, producing uncoordinated blur. More dope comes our way, via an anorexic speedball in a Christmas cocktail outfit, the pub's theme bra strapped on over her top. She's shivering, even in this sauna, diamanté baubles clinking on the bra. Would we like to peddle dope with her? No, we would not; Yvonne doesn't like it either, dope makes her think of nothing but sex. The girl asks if we can hear the superwoofer—they've just had it installed.

"Ohhhh, yes," says Yvonne. "YEeesss." She's off the superwoofer now and on to *memory*. She once drove stoned for hours with Robbie, couldn't even communicate her sexual fantasies because they were all so fluid and so exhausting. "Ahhhh!" She flicks her hair, offering me a hand. "May I have the pleasure?"

"No thanks, I can't, I'll get some drinks."

"Ooooh." She bashes her hand against her forehead. "Oh no. Sorry, I forgot, you're on duty, aren't you. Oh, yes."

She softens, baby pats my hair, feet stomping a flamenco exit. I watch hazy waitresses come and go, more themed bras worn over T-shirts, slung around necks. Humorous, I'm not, my eyes are on Ruth, filling with something approaching anger.

I struggle with the drinks; a sweat to get them, a sweat to take them back.

I glimpse Meryl and Ruth dancing flirtatiously, they're joined by a freaky thin man wearing a tinsel-encrusted baby pouch with a short-haired dog inside. Another couple are seminaked, glittering torsos, rubber reindeer horns on their heads. Ruth spies me or, I suspect, the drinks and comes bouncing on over. She downs a beer without asking. She is winding me up. I grab the spare bottle.

"Can you get me another one?"

"No, I don't think you should be drinking."

"Well, I think I should."

The tone is Meryl's, non-negotiable. She wiggles back to Meryl's side and whispers in her ear, Meryl's hand lightly strokes Ruth's arm, all the way down and around the wrist, very, very, lightly—deliberately done. I feel it, I touch my own arm, my hand feels rough. They separate, Meryl heading for the bar.

It's after eleven, more and more people are pumping into the bar, I rise in panic. Applause for house band, where is she? Where is she? Clap, clap, clap, this place is hot, I'm too fucking old for this, too many people for proper surveillance. Everytime I sight Ruth my view is blocked by writhing glitter babes. I'm forced to join Yvonne on the dance floor, subtly manoeuvring my way next to Ruth, who incidentally is having her ear expertly kissed by Meryl. Far too far . . . it freaks me out. I push on over to Yani.

"Hi."

"Hi." He dances on beside me, can't hear so I have to tap him on the shoulder, shout into his ear.

"What's with your sister?"

He tiptoes up and looks in their direction. Meryl's passionately kissing Ruth.

He shouts, "She fancies Ruth."

"That's kind of irresponsible," I say.

Tim bops to Yani, who shouts my concerns at Tim. They both shrug back, they don't see why.

"Yes why?"

Tim laughs at me, "Are you homophobic?"

I laugh right back at him. Here I am protecting *his* sister, who's still, by the way, in the grip of a delusional faith, her will in tatters. Where anything could happen, we have recordings, we have proof. Oh, quit it. My arms are folded, my eyes focusing on nothing in particular, jostled about between bodies on the floor.

I go ask Robbie for the car keys, he taps his cigarette in an ash-producing gesture and dangles them above my head: progress.

Ruth is now no longer where she was, or at the bar, I push through jumping bodies towards Meryl.

"Excuse me Meryl, where's Ruth?"

No response. My eyes are buzzing.

"Excuse me Meryl, where's Ruth?"

"I heard you and I'm thinking." Long pause, while Meryl assesses me. *She knows? She doesn't know? What the fuck is going on?* More pause while I *fail.* . . . She wants me to beg. Sweating and twitching with a half-nervy smile, I jig my feet 'round in front of her. When she speaks, she speaks in slow motion: "She wanted some air."

The street light is low, she could be hiding anywhere, everywhere . . . Ohh shit don't panic. Panic. I run around to where we parked, she isn't by the car. I run back towards the bar, stop, listen—hear talking, laughing. Run left to where the voices come from. Dope-saturated air, follow it 'round the back of the bar to a group of weirdos partying. Ruth's sitting in her bra, head propped against the dog freak's chest, she's guzzling from a bottle, held by him. His hand sneaks down her bra releasing a breast. He bends down and gives himself a little suck. I feel drawn, repelled, watching him handle the left breast, which is left hanging as he drinks more beer. Another individual sticks his hand up her skirt, pulling at her leggings. He's so in there getting them off, my tugs confuse him, he wants them down. I pull them up. The bigger boy staggers up grabbing at my arm. I shake him off. "Ruth, where's your top?"

"Hello Daddy."

"Ruth, where's your top?"

The dog boy tugs at me. "Hey you ol' bastard, we brought her beer."

"Did you?"

"Yeees." In front of me he starts to suck her breast.

"Ruth, we should go."

"Hi Daddy." She looks at me, "I want to fuck you, Daddy. Come on Daddy. Daddy FUCK ME!!!"

"Shush. Hey, stop that Ruth." I pull her up. She falls against stocky boy, he kicks out, missing me.

"She's sick," I say.

"Everyone's sick," he says.

I feel a hand on my pocket, a little deeper, little deeper. Whack! I slap down hard across his hand. He wants a drink. "Please?" Yeah, *please!* I throw him a twenty, he hoots out happy after it, fingers scrambling through the dirt. We can't find Ruth's top, she thinks Meryl's got it. She didn't love it anyway and we're almost at the car, but she wants to speak to Meryl.

"I've got to speak to Meryl."

"You need to lie down."

"No, Meryl needs me, I have to talk to her."

"No you don't, you need to go home."

I open the car door, go back to usher her in, gently by the elbow. We're almost there, almost, when she breaks free.

"No don't!"

"I'm helping you, Ruth."

She looks at me strange, checks down at her leggings. I move forward. "No, no, No! DON'T!" she says. Then, louder, "Help!! Help me, HELP!!! Rape. Rape!!"

I yell: "Stop it! Don't be so goddamned selfish!"

She doesn't stop, she sits down and inhales deeply, her mouth opens.

"SHUT UP!" I put my hand across her mouth, she's kicking me, my hand grips tighter round her jaw. I twist her arm, it hurts her, I don't care. Twisting and dragging her body towards the car, she goes stiff, makes her easier to pull. I throw her into the back seat, hoping it does hurt, I want to hurt her. She flops, slides along the seat, her eyelids drop. I have to sit, my body's trembling, my hands won't function on the keys. Fuzzy kinds of tremble, inside my muscles, that *Rape! Rape!* ringing in my ears.

Out on the road it's pitch black, I'm fumbling for the beam. There's nothing on the road, which is kind of eerie. It's hot, no air-conditioning, no water. My hands tighten round the wheel. Jealousy. Some chasm opened for me back there in that nightclub, placed me right there on the edge. I couldn't take anyone touching her. A car's coming up behind me and another one after that. The first one passes me on full beam, the other decides to tailgate. Ruth's slumped down across the backseat, sleeping. I take out my handkerchief and wipe my face; turn on the radio, no station, only two turn-offs second on the left. The car behind stays glued all the way to the intersection.

17

What scared me most was the awful knowing I couldn't leave him, I couldn't will myself to finally escape. It wasn't planned, I started up too late for that. The words were in my mouth, I tried to shout them, I said the "rapes" out loud, but couldn't concentrate enough to completely scream. I gave up. It wasn't just his hand smothering my words. I felt a paralysis in my throat. To have forgotten something so basic got me scared. I thought maybe he had heard my fear in some strange psychic way, but he couldn't have because he was just looking at me and wrestling with my body.

The car is whooshing through the night—I pretend to sleep. My mind is travelling in two places, one mind's destructive, the other's not. The destructive one's going. It's all lost, it's all over, your faith is fucked, there is nothing out there, all there is is fantasy and the grand no-purpose reality. We live, we die, we fuck, get on with it. The positive side's saying, No, you're not destroyed, he's only one person. There are mad gurus out there, Baba may be mad, so what? It doesn't mean the whole experience is crap.

I feel revolted trading sex for soul. The good side says that, that was bad, you didn't need to do it. The negative says, That was great, you really showed him the true face of his pussy religion. You found his weakness and drove on through it.

It's also saying, You're a big coward and a slag for not trying to escape. I try the door, the central locking's off. I ease down the handle and push, the ground rushes up immediately and I feel nauseous, my eyes half shut, half pulling at the door. PJ leans over and slams it hard. I close my eyes again and feel even sicker. I tell him he has to pull over or I'll throw up in the car.

We arrive back at the hut. Again, neither of us had left a light on. I can't even see my way through, must be 2:00 a.m., it's dark, dark. PJ has to guide me in, I let him, I just want to sleep. The hut's simple and warm—I flake. PJ puts a flannel on my head. I wake full of sinister lonely thoughts. I've committed some terrible crime; there's a man and a woman, in a car. He's killed her with a rock and we have to bury her and try to erase the memory. I get up, half convinced I've helped murder this woman.

It's about 3:20. PJ's awake, he's made tea and pours it out. He knows now what I take, milk; I watch it swirling, grease spots on the top. I look at him all smiley and say, "Thank you," and "I want to go home."

"Well you can't."

"Why not, I'm cured, I can drink, fuck, and dance."

"Because you're out of control."

"You didn't seem to mind last night. Come on it's over. You're fucked."

He sips his tea, "No, it's not over. For one thing you've been drinking, and two, we're still in the cave. But now it's a much darker, deeper cave than it was last night."

"Ooo, scary."

"Yes and I've seen people scramble their brains over less than this."

He thinks we're accomplices, bound by our mutual whoring. Ooooh, this is what's wrong with talking, it gets you going so you blah on, hoping they'll stop blahing back. Blah, blah.

"All right! I'll admit it! In India I was influenced by processes beyond my control."

He sort of blows his cheeks out. I know what he's doing: he's just trying to deny the sex and blame Baba. I slide off the couch and crawl 'round to him on all fours, flopping my big paws onto his knees.

"Meow." I smile up into his face. "Happy? I'm happy, what about you?"

I reach out for his sandy old cheek, ooh he's so grumpy, he shifts my elbows off his knees, crosses his legs. I'm definitely getting the stern old dial.

"You're playing with me, Ruth."

"How?"

"Shut up." He smiles at me. "If you want to play with power, take my chair."

I shift about. . . .

"Well go on, take it."

Humm, I get up first, he stands up too and we pass in front of the coffee table, sideways, so close I almost knock him over. It doesn't feel that different in his seat. I feel self-conscious, pretending and squeezing the arms. In truth I'm not sure I do feel more powerful, or anything. It just feels like me in a different chair.

"Well, go on, use your power."

I sit up straight.

"All right then, I want to know what you like best about me. Do you like my personality? Or do you like my breasts best?"

"Is that supposed to be funny?"

"No."

He chortles to himself, rubs his hands, and stares at me—unnecessarily long.

"Okay, right now Ruth, I like your breasts best, it's just the way it is. You can't stop me or any other grizzly old geezer having sexual thoughts about you. You're there, and I think about you."

"Oh yes, and what are your thoughts?"

"They're private."

"Not the other night."

He sets his tea down and fills the cup.

"And how was it for you?"

I press my lips together. "Hummmm. It was a bit revolting."

He nods, he's nodding, his finger taps at the rim of

his cup. He moves it twice. Deliberately. Eyes focused down at cup level.

"You're a bitch," he says, still looking at his cup.

"All right," I say. "It was interesting historically: *Oh babe, come babe.* I haven't heard that before."

There's a deep intake of air. The fingernail taps, I fidget with a mozzie coil, it breaks up in my hands.

"Listen, young lady, I had sex with you because you begged me to. Now if you think it's funny to insult me, then I think you're a cruel and stupid young woman."

He's looking straight at me, his forehead develops shooting lines, they crease around his eyebrows. I sigh, running my finger 'round the inside of my bra. There's a red indentation along the top of my breasts, I trace it with my fingers and start to undo my bra, it's sort of engrossing, freeing the damp patches, rubbing and spreading them. I go over and squat next to him, very close to his face, my breasts practically touching his nose.

"What about you kiss me?"

"Really?"

"Yes."

I bob my breasts around his eyes, just touching. I don't really like this, but Robbie says it drives men wild with smothering ideas, the idea of being smothered by beautiful soft mammaries. I push them hard into his face. Sandpaper, creepy, he touches them, makes them tickly.

I pull back and cup my hands over the nipples. "Let's see if I can teach you."

He's all huffy and sulks. Slides his eyes to the wall. "I know how to do it!"

"I don't think so," I say, "not so I like it. I want you to take off my pants and do it slowly."

He smiles at me, okay, okay, all keen for the game. He gets down and kneels up in front of me. He hesitates. For a minute he does nothing but breathe on my stomach. Then he slides his hands up under my leggings, hooks his thumbs into the elastic, and pulls down my pants so slowly that the sensation interests me. Just as I'm thinking this he buries his face roughly in my pubic hair. It hurts, it's so forceful and prickly! I shove his head back.

"No. No, don't. Kiss all around it gently."

When he starts back in it's too gentle, an eyelash, butterfly kiss. I say, "Just kiss it normally," and pull his head in and move it 'round. He kisses for ages 'round the outside, all the bits that don't *normally* get done. I tell him to take the leggings off. He crawls round behind me and rolls them to my knees. He stays there—I feel strange and hot not knowing what he'll do, my buttocks spread apart, he spreads them anatomically as if he were a doctor and pushes them back together again, he does this a few times, then holds them open and tries to slip his tongue in.

"Hey, I don't like that, take the leggings right off."

He rolls them down my legs and helps them past my feet.

"Lie down."

I almost do this, then I remember who's in charge. "No, you. You go into the bedroom . . . ." He takes some steps to the bedroom, turns to see where I am.

I say, "Why are you waiting?"

"I was waiting for you."

"Well don't wait. Take your clothes off and lie down."

He stops for a moment and then strips quite sure and butch. I like his tree-trunk legs. I've always been attracted to thunder thighs, it's the thought of what that strength could do to you. They're like delicious trees. I decide I have to do this, go down and feel them—they do feel good, my hands travel up and down, it's the only reason I watch sports on television, it gratifies my heinous fantasies. I imagine how those muscles could squash and obliterate me and how I could squeeze and abuse them back.

I don't really know what I'm doing but it occurs to me that I should. So I tell him I've changed my mind, I want him to massage my back. I lie down on the bed and he begins. It's a strange back massage because I can feel his desire and fury through his hands. I love it. I love the warmth and the fact that I've demanded him to do it. He's really very attentive in an odd hateful sort of way. He turns me over and spreads my legs, his fingers rush for my cunt and try to thrust inside, I put my hands down and tell him, "No, don't."

He says he can't stop, he needs to come inside me.

I say, "Look, it's not good enough having you thrusting inside me. I want to feel as if you're a strong, overpowering masseur, who's slowly undoing all the knots in my body. I want you releasing every layer in me . . . Do you understand?"

He doesn't speak, he starts massaging my stomach with his palms in circles, then breaks off, kneading my stomach and thighs with his knuckles. He pulls my legs apart so he can massage round the crease at the top of my thighs. I let him flop my legs about—it's relaxing. He massages my cold feet. I used to think if I were queen that's what I'd hire, a permanent foot masseuse. The sensation is such bliss I don't want it to stop. He places a pillow underneath my bottom and lazily strums his fingers along my pubic patch. He parts me and blows, which I'm not sure I like, the exposure sort of leaves me in midair. He puts his lips down inside me as I'm still trying to decide what should happen next—whether it should be my decision or his. I feel his tongue very hot against me, he's obviously done this before, there's no teeth grinding or tongue stabbing, it's pleasurable and I can't be bothered attacking him or myself any longer. I want the oblivion, down here in this hut where no one can see us, I don't care.

After sex I ask, "How am I going to keep the balance?"

He doesn't understand.

"You know, the inner balance, the balance inside myself."

"Between what and what?"

"Between negative and positive, good and bad."

"You mean you don't know the difference?"

"Of course I know the bloody difference."

"Ha ha. You mean you don't want the responsibility."

Ha ha. What a bastard.

The morning was mad. I woke alone on the couch, how I don't know. And there was someone else there, in the hut, walking in heels, I could hear them clacking across the floor. I played dead. Clack, clack, clack, then over to me, clacky clack. My hair was gently lifted from my face. "Oh yes," the woman whispered. I felt the sheet lift as she inspected my body then fall as she tucked me in. Her hands were soft and sure, she smelt of peppermints. As she left, I opened my eyes, her calves were plump and black. I could hear her talking in a Yankee accent out by the shower. Shit she was serious.

I crept out and hid behind the window, she was giving PJ heaps, some blah about the phone. Her bum wiggled as she poked him in the chest, she was an attractive chunky with fierce eyes and a stiff Cleopatra hairdo.

PJ's apologising, he was going to call.

"When?"

"When I'd finished."

"Have you finished?"

"Yes pretty much, she's pretty much there. . . . I was—Hey! I had enough to worry about without thinking who in the hell's getting the fucking phone."

"Don't you. . ." (something, something) ". . . go chewing your stuff out on me, pal. You're incredible. I can't believe what I'm seeing 'round here. She's got you, hasn't she? She's in there totally manipulating things with you and I just wonder how come she can. I just w—"

A car door slams out in front. I don't want to talk, so I throw myself back naked on the couch. Robbie is calling out, "Carol, Carol?" He comes on in, tiptoes over when he sees me and stands, stays, ogling down at me for—what seems like agonisingly—ever, then wanders off towards the bedroom. The fridge door opens, he drinks something from a bottle and lights a cigarette. The woman calls out his name and he leaves. I get up, pull on a top, last night's leggings.

PJ comes in, rinses his hanky, brings it over, dripping wet, with a plate of sandwiches.

"Well," I say. "So who was that?"

"Carol Phelps."

"And?"

"And she lives with me."

"Oh. Great."

"I didn't think she was going to come."

"Tee, hee, I bet she wanted to smack your arse."

"I suppose that would have appealed to your sadistic nature."

"Yes it would, you should have heard her. She was clack, clacking away in her shoes, looking down at me, muttering things. I'm acting asleep, then she tucked me in like a baby."

"Well, you are a little baby, aren't you?"

Hmmm. I sit up, we share his sandwich. He looks refreshed, and that annoys me.

"Yes, and you should be sleeping with girlies your own age, then you wouldn't have to stick dye an' shit in your hair."

I stuff down more sandwich, he passes me a paper serviette nice as pie and says, "Man hater."

Boy! I scoff, look up, put down the sandwich, and blush. Why am I blushing? He says an out-of-the-way bitchy thing to me and I'm blushing. My insides go cold with anger.

"Well, that would be convenient, wouldn't it?"

Pause. Eyeball, blink.

He leaps up and grabs at my wrist, I scream, he laughs at me, walks two paces, then lies down on the floor. He's laughing so much, he's dabbing at his eyes.

"Haaaaaaah. Hah. Okay Ruth, I want you to do your worst. I'm going to lie down here and I want to hear it all. Your absolute, uncensored worst."

He wriggles over, puts his head right by my feet, I feel obliged to tuck them up in case I kick him in the head.

I look down, he's smiling up, all expectant . . . waiting. All right, I think. I will.

"Okay Tampax tool, I'm going to give it to you. All this man-hating shit for a start. *Oh dear, she criticised me so I'll call her a man hater. . . . that'll screw her up.* It's just crap. It's just so obvious I don't know what to do with it. I know what you want from me. . . . You want a youthful pussy transfusion, preferably one you can take back home and show all the menfolk what a beautiful post you got to piss on. Mr. Pressed Jeans and Cowboy Boots, is that a uniform for individuals, is it?"

PJ has his eyes shut, still preserving the big fixed smile. I roll off the sofa onto his stomach, thinking I'll bounce off in a dignified landing. I miss. He's groaning and moaning, I'm giggling, rolling around beside him. We sort of pause and look, he snuggles into me, tries to kiss me.

"No don't," I say, breathing into his face. "I want a young man."

His eyes crinkle up and stay there, he's not laughing now. He turns and looks at me, I glare back, he pinches my cheek, hard.

"Your physical superiority makes you unkind."

"Yes, it does, and it's the whole reason we're talking intimate, as in *Salivating old slob requires slim young thing.*" I rub my cheek, he turns to me. "Okay, okay."

"No!" I thump his chest. "I haven't finished yet! Old salivating slob seeks slim young thing for stimulating conversation. . . . *Excuse me dear while I part the meat curtains.*"

His face is stony. "Jesus, Ruth, I don't use language like that."

"No?"

"No."

I deep sigh, he taps my hand. "Keep it going."

"That's it."

"You're holding back."

"No, I'm not. I'm not." He's right, I am. There was another memorable phrase—piss flaps—and even in my head I have to hold my breath and say it very tiny. Like I don't want them to be there, the words . . . used by a male lecturer. Only to his male students, of course. But I just can't bring myself to repeat them and have to hear those words out loud.

PJ tentatively touches my shoulder. "Ruth, I'm disappointed."

"Well yes, I know, I'm thinking . . . If I do more things to you, you'll just get off on it."

"It's a risk you'll have to take."

"Maybe I'll sit on you then."

I do, I sit on his chest, patting away the sweat and massaging his face into shapes. I suppose I could tie a string round his penis and lead him out on a walk . . . Nooo. Too silly. It's funny, I just can't get a fix on what to do with him. His face is relaxed, features distorting back and forth.

"I've got it!"

"What?"

"I know what you need." I stroke his hair back. "Don't move!"

Shit, shit, it's brilliant. My hands begin to shake slightly as they push off his chest. In the bedroom I hunt through makeup and clothes. . . . I'm panting with vision. Men don't take care of their skin, there's always stray bristles on their noses, eyebrows, everywhere, so I'll fix those first. He squeals as he's plucked. The thick ones are trophies—I hold them up, he's not impressed. He doesn't want to see. His skin looks good with makeup, all the imperfections go. It needs loose powder, he has a T-zone oily area, we've only got compact powder, which is caked. His breathing gets very long, people fussing over you does that, you trance out into never-never land. I used to get a teacher to do it, she'd lean in over my shoulder, her hand busy scribbling away, while I went numb with pleasure.

He stands in plain black briefs, a square of sun hitting him through the window. He wants to peek, but I won't let him. I want the full effect, Yvonne's purple knitted top, Mum's elasticated batik skirt. The top's straining over his arms, exposing almost all his navel. I quite like the look of butch drag. I'd love it if all those city blokes in Sydney or Fifth Avenue would wear sexy skirts and midriff tops.

"You know you look lovely, sexy."

"Stop it."

"No, come on, I want to show you."

He walks up and takes my hand, complete obedience—worry, worry, hee hee—he seems to be enjoying himself. Critically, I don't think he'd pass as a woman, he'd be indexed under Tough Old Dears. We gaze at the mirror. I've forgotten lipstick, he has to have lipstick. I apply copper-coloured eyeshadow. He's pulling odd faces in the mirror. I stroke his cheek and murmur, "Look—a same-age fun-loving woman, *bet your scones are dynamite.*" He lunges at me, planting big tongue kisses on my face.

"Oh don't, you old leso, don't. Oow, you're so aggressive, stop it."

He bear hugs me and sucks my lips abruptly, tugging at them.

"Fuck you, Ruth." Smack, smack.

"Ouch." I wipe my lips, which hurt. "No, you fuck yourself, except you wouldn't, would you!"

I go out and sulk on the sofa. He follows, flopping into the armchair, legs crossed, foot jerking towards me, nudging at my shin.

"I was young once, and handsome too, you'd have been impressed."

"I wasn't born."

We look at each other. Me at my creation, him at his. I'm going. I jump up before he can stop me; run out of the hut, slamming the door. His feet thud up behind me, he opens the door—and I'm standing there, feet completely on the threshold, staring straight at him, eyeball to eyeball. He folds his arms, nodding.

I laugh, "Hee, hee, I won didn't I? I'm on top, aren't I? I'm the winner." My fists beat against his chest. "Ahhhhhhhh."

"Yes, you won, Ruth."

"AHHHHHH." My feet pound out a victory dance, up and down and 'round in front of him, jumping, twisting, and pounding. My voice shrieks as I scream nonsense congratulations. "Yes, yes, yes!!" I shout across to PJ "So what are you! Say it!"

"A dirty old man."

He comes on over to me, smiling. Slips his arms around my waist, we jump 'round and 'round together till we're tired of it and can't. I pant like a dog.

"God! I wish my friends were here, we could have a good laugh, this is such bloody fun. Ohh haaah, ha. Sooo . . ." We pause, I pat him on the shoulder. "So tell me PJ, what am I?"

As soon as I've said it, I'm nervous. He stops laughing and assesses me, it's awkward. He doesn't say anything, I scratch my head.

"Well?"

"I'd like to write it on your forehead."

"Why?"

"Because if I just tell you, you might be disappointed."

In the kitchen he tries out a biro—it doesn't work. I laugh, he scribbles with it on a bag. My hair is pulled right back as he presses with it on my forehead, the point feels sharp. Two letters, six letters. He goes over and over them.

"It's nothing horrid, is it?"

"Surprise."

He leads me through to the bedroom, our bedroom, the one we slept in. I'm suddenly frightened and pull away.

"If it's something sick you have to tell me."

"It's not."

I look in the mirror, the words are back to front, mirror language.

"Oh great, what's it say?"

I squint into the bloody mirror. BEEE . . . Bee.

He interrupts me, tickling, annoying me, he knows I'm really keen. B-e . . . be . . .

He hands me my makeup compact. I sort of crane 'round to check. B-e K-I-N-D. Be kind.

"So what? Don't you think I'm kind?"

"No I don't."

We're looking into the mirror, bnix əꓭ wobbling out at us. We look more acceptable in the mirror, drag queen and prisoner.

"But you're supposed to say what I am. For Godsake, now I feel bad. Why couldn't you just write 'Cruel'?"

I trace the letters with my fingers, he says, "Hey come on, Ruth." But I can't, I can't come on. I go and walk about in the lounge."

"No, you're right. Be kind, that's the whole point.

Thank you, I'm very grateful, this is it, isn't it? The only thing. The Dalai Lama says it, kindness. 'My religion is kindness.' You'd think he'd say something unbearably profound, wouldn't you?"

I slump down on the couch, I can barely hold my body up. He's following me 'round, his skirt swishing, sitting legs apart so you can see right up it. I sit, deep in brood, thinking dark, heavy thoughts.

"Do you know what I'm really scared of?"

"What?"

"I don't want you to tell anybody."

"I won't."

I look at him, hearing myself breathing, thinking what I'm going to say, "I'm scared . . ."

"Yes?"

"Well I'm scared that, despite all my strong feelings, I'm really heartless."

He grins at me, looking leery.

"Well?"

"Well," he says, lifting his hands and ruffling his hair. "I was hoping you'd be heartless enough to abuse me for your own sick pleasure."

18

We're in the bedroom, I'm lying on the bed. Ruth kneels beside me bashing at my chest, thump, thump. THUMP! I cup her breast, this is not met with amusement, my hand is slapped away, the better to focus on herself.

"Ruth, keep it light."

"No, I don't want light, I want all the stuff that isn't light."

"Groan."

"Yes, groan!"

I kiss her neck, which she allows, her neck held tense under my lips. I kiss again, she pays little attention, still morosely introspective.

"It's not a joke," she says. "You said it yourself, no one can be close to me."

She lies back on the pillows, breathing in her resentment, sighing it out in long depressed pangs. I kiss her shoulder, thinking you can't cure everything with words—apparently not her impression. When I foolishly express this terminal cliché out loud, she goes, "Oooh, Ohh, no," too disgruntled to even swear.

The sheet is rolled into a lumpy divider, tunnelled down the bed between us.

"Well," she says, wriggling her back, "I haven't finished with words."

"All right, you tell me."

"I want to know if you even like me?"

This is not a good question, how I answer this could seriously disrupt my chances of making love to her again. She waits for the personality download, eyes ominously cool. Her directness bothers me, I realise she's ahead, aware I want to fuck her, so if I fudge around telling her lies she won't make love to me anyway.

"Look, Ruth, you're perfectly good, mostly, as you are."

"But do you like me?"

She adopts a militant pose, arms folded, eyes set ahead, not an invitation to truth.

"I don't know, I like that you're brave."

"Yes," she agrees, she likes that too.

I take her hand and massage it carefully, kissing all her fingers. She enjoys this and gives me her arm. I massage up the arm and onto the breast. Then get up, unravel the sheet, climb back in, hugging and kissing her underneath. She fumbles in the skirt for my penis. She says she likes a "tubby penis" and flops it round. She tells me she wants us to be in a black room, no light at all, and would I mind?

I say, "No," too eagerly, my body swelling with curiosity, heart aching to please. I'm told I'm supposed to embody a stranger who doesn't talk at all. Nothing's explicit but I get subliminal inklings I'm to be dominant hooker.

This takes some minutes to prepare, I have to arrange blankets over the blinds, another one under the door. A ball of twisted paper inserted into the keyhole and it becomes pitch black, even when the eyes adjust you can't actually see. I reach out and find a leg, my hands wander up it, spreading out at the top of her thigh, my hand stretches out full width over her pussy. The hair's very nice to stroke, a wiry soft texture, I'm stroking down, very softly down, careful not to go instantly inside her. When my fingers do reach in I run them loosely down either side, exploring in the same direction, gently pulling at the plump wet folds, then I slip down further and massage 'round her anus. I don't put my fingers into her, in fact when I move down to kiss there I can't see anything at all.

It's kind of pornographic and makes me think of pornographic things. The girl in a Truffaut movie talking about rough licks she had from cows in the cow shed, long flat strokes all the way up and all the way down. There's another scene where the same girl wrestles with three pimps in a parking lot. They pull her into the back of the car over the pimp boss's knee, he sits upright in his black leather gloves, clinically patting at her backside, tugging up her skirt, exposing an extra thin pair of nylon pants. He picks at them, slapping, testing her resistance with bigger slaps—she doesn't move. He spanks her harder, dishing out a precisely measured walloping before he lets her go.

I feel Ruth responding under me in little jerks. I twist her legs, so she's lying on her front, I sit on her two beautiful buttocks and rub myself into them. My hands move along her back, pressing more and more air out of her lungs. I reach down, under her breasts, lifting her torso towards me, stretching her back. I'm doing this to slow me down, it's lifesaving, you push down and pull the shoulders back. If I don't do this now I'll just come, and curl up next to her. I turn her over and kiss her on the mouth. It's a relief not to see, to be selfish and not worry about her, to just feel my way, having angry and loving thoughts. The images of dominance wander off in a rush of warmth; I don't even know where it begins, I suppose in the genitals, wherever it starts the feeling continues in a helpless wave. I start thinking only of her. My body wants to please her so much I'm almost lost, forgetting my usual repertoire. I settle on top of her, wriggling in. This takes concentration without my hands, my hands want to calm her, stroke her, acknowledge the heat from her. She feels down herself guiding me in. When I'm in I try not to think of her, putting all my effort into "NOT." Not coming, not kissing, not hugging, I think of Carol, deserts, and freezing lakes.

She breaks her silence and says, "Pull out."

I do, I lie beside her, she holds my hand, waiting, touching my brow drawing on it with her fingers, little snake patterns and whorls. Then she moves up astride me, sitting completely still. When I try to move she stops me, her hands rotate on my chest, up around my neck. My neck gets very tense, always has, separates two warring factions, head from body. She rocks incredibly slowly, so connected I'm hardly conscious. She leans forward, breasts bobbing on my chest, again very lightly, so light I don't feel she's with me. Then when her lips press and we kiss, I feel she's only thinking of me.

Hmmmm, I'm imagining Ruth as wife without the picket fence and apron. Ruth as travelling companion, life partner, opening the last remaining doors to my psyche. I lean over and pat in the general direction of her face. Which is wet—from crying? "Have you been crying?" No response. "Are you okay there?"

"Yeah."

"You're not upset?"

"I'm having an emotion."

"Something bad?"

"No. Yes and no."

"I'm fantasising about you."

"Well don't."

"I love you."

"Ohh don't, don't . . . spoil it."

"Do you love me?"

"Ohh YOU! Do you really have to ask me?"

"Yes, I guess I do, I am asking you."

"Well I'm not answering, it's just too stupid."

She snorts, chuckles, snorts, pulls my hand away from her face puts it between her legs, on top of her pubic hair as a kind of extra quilt.

"OOOF."

"What?"

"Ooof, nothing. I'm just thinking. What am I going to do now? That's all, at least with the enlightenment I felt I was moving out of the mud. My mucky mud."

I seek out her hand, it's damp and tense.

"Do you want me to take the blankets down?"

"Ooof, no, too much."

She starts giggling away next to me. "With my luck, he'd probably shrivel up."

"Who?"

"My next *genuine* Indian master, the one who's going to pull the string out of my head."

She sniffs and removes her hand.

"What were your goals before you went to India?"

"Hee hee, can't remember."

"Yes you can."

"Oh," sigh, "work," sigh, "finish University," sigh. "Go into the city, work, set up with Tim."

"What's wrong with that?"

"Just money, crap."

"Did you feel that way before you went?"

"I didn't sort of feel too much."

I sleep and wake in a sweat with all the bedclothes on top of me. Ruth isn't there, I doze back and suddenly see myself alone and panicked in the hut. That gets me up, perspiration running everywhere, blankets still up, blackout, no idea of time—DAY, even! My feet rummage across the floor with poor results; no shoes, no jeans, hoisting myself back into the freakin' skirt. Open the door—ohh, the relief of having fresh air circulate. Ruth's up dressed in an odd assortment of dishcloths and shirt. There's a stack of paperback books in front of her, a knife, and a sheet. The sheet is being attacked, slashed at, by the knife. She's tearing the sheet into strips. I go to the sink and—puke—there's a large grey spider in the tray, the size of a goddamn hand. Small body, with thin weedy legs going out like buttresses, raising the whole putrid thing off the bottom like stilts. It sits there throbbing, I don't feel I can kill it, or reach down under it with my hands. The thought creeps me out, so I push the mop handle down under the body, hoping the legs will tentatively walk aboard. They do. It stops and clings so I raise the handle slowly, making for the door. As soon as the handle's horizontal the spider animates, scuttling back up towards my hand. I vigorously shake the mop out, thinking it will drop, no action. Then—Wham! The damn thing hurtles itself towards me. I throw the handle down, half splatting the spider against the floor. Ruth comes over and examines it, still moving, dragging its badly squished body across the floor. She tuts over the spider, tapping it dead.

"You should have used paper." She scoops the spider up between two paperbacks and flicks it out the door. I stare out after it—minuscule . . . now it's been crushed and battered in.

I go to the fridge for mineral water, take a long cool slug. Ruth's furiously ripping and tearing material behind me, I ask her what she's doing. She doesn't answer my question specifically, skips on to a statement of her own.

"It's over," she says.

I look up as if she's crazy and didn't say it. Don't know what to do. Go over and perch beside the sofa. Watching her hands working away, rolling up the material into what looks like bandages. Noticing the slightly damp hair—she must have showered and been up some time. I'm probably lucky she hasn't already bolted. Bolted, into the blue, blue sky, which is how it's been ever since I got here. I'm gazing out at the sky for answers. I can't say, You're not going, so I say,

"No, it's not . . . It's not over."

She sighs, and continues winding, makes me feel listless, incapacitated. Her eyes, the hand, shape of her mouth, they all turn me on, that spider was her and I can't fucking well handle either of them. She's shaking her head, in deep consternation, deep something.

She says, "Look. Look, it's all gone, I'm ashamed of myself. I tortured you, it was all a defilement."

"But I liked it, I think we should be together."

"Together, NO . . . for Christsake."

I smile at her in a sickly desperate way, I can't stop myself from smiling, she must sense my desperation sweating out in drops. It's also (I remind myself) her shift in faith. You doubt, you doubt everything.

"Here, you need some water, you'll dehydrate."

She takes the bottle from me, drinks, and puts it by her feet.

"I thought there was something good happening here?"

"Ooh. Yes. But I don't want commitment, I'm too young. I'm really, really young and superficial, I don't know how to love anyone."

She looks distressed, places three paperbacks under her left foot and starts winding and binding the damned sheeting round her foot.

"Hey, hey stop it, Ruth. Come on. What is it really?"

She sits up and stares at me.

"I'm fed up. I'm lost. And this is a bloody wilderness. We would never, ever, have been together in the outside world, we wouldn't have met."

I go over to the chair, touch her, take her hand in mine. "But that's the beauty of it, isn't it? The miracle of meeting."

She pulls her hand away, returning to the paperbacks.

I lean down with her, whisper in her ear, "I can help you grow."

"You already have."

"No, I can do more . . . much more. I can eliminate the crap. Have you functioning entirely in the present."

She's not fully listening, working on her other foot.

"What about Carol?"

"Carol can't handle me." I pull her hand to my lips. Kiss, kiss.

"Look Ruth, I know what you're thinking because we all think the same. We all think there'll be hundreds of people out there for us. Hundreds of people we could truly love. Whereas in reality there may be only three."

She eases out her hand, wipes it on a tea towel. Rocks back and forth on the couch; her eyes turn on me. Silence, then: "Go look at yourself. Get changed. It's over, it started wrong and it just got worse!"

The rocking's kind of infectious, I move up and down with her, watch her eye my outfit. It's a pretty sad outfit. I laugh, Ruth doesn't find it funny, tears running down her cheeks. She gets up, agitated, high-stepping it about the hut. The door, the sink, the door, I try to stay calm but can't.

"No, Ruth, don't!"

I end up running for the door, grabbing at her hand. She shakes it off, shakes me off. I sink down, my arms clasping 'round her ankles.

"Why don't we get married."

"No, don't, please don't, you're mad."

She squats down beside me, bending back my thumbs, sweating. We both sweat. She says she's had enough and to let her go. She pinches me and moves away. I ask her to stop. "Stop!" I can see she's very frightened, doesn't want me, doesn't believe I love her, doesn't want to stop. She's not going to stop, she slips out the door. I follow barefoot, feeling the hard rocks, too tightly wound to pay attention. "Come on, give us a chance." I take her hand and dance in the desert, ridiculous, beautiful. I'd be laughing, I almost am but am too fucking desperate, horribly tight. For a moment I think I have her, she's moving with me in the brilliant light.

I pull up, blinded. She's walking fast, jogging from me, step-hobbling to the car, past the car. . . . She bends to check her paperbacks. There's a small log lying halfway between us, smooth, bleached, wispy branch to one side. She's crouched, one knee up, untying and retying her knots. I stare at the log, I know I'll pick it up. My eyes are on her head, the back of her very round head. I raise the log, my arm floats up on automatic. . . . There's a sound, not a loud sound, a dull *thunk*. She's leaning, reaching, holding onto my arm, trying to steady herself, looking into my eyes, slipping down, her legs crumpling. I'm cradling her head. She looks like an animal does when it's hurt: no noise, no complaint, a look of perfect trust. Then her focus falls back inside herself and her eyelids close.

Oh baby, baby please wake up. You'll be better, you'll be fine.

I lay her out on the sofa, and am preparing a cold flannel, wrapping up ice cubes with trembling hands.

She has indentation marks on her head. I dab at them, placing the flannel lightly across her forehead. Very, very, faintly I hear a hum, a car noise. A car with no horns; it's definitely there, they don't want me to know either. If we'd been talking, I wouldn't have heard.

I can't find the car keys. Usually I have designated orderly places, like by the door, first drawer on the dressing table. I check those places anyway—nothing. Shit. What the hell have I done with them? I can't remember, can't visualise them, trying to force this starts a head buzz. Gotta think, can't think; check the top of the fridge, window ledges, bench, back of sofa, chair . . . everything. Sweat spreads along my armpits. I check the car, they're not in the ignition. I'm about to explode when I spot them on the dash—glinting, red-hot. I go back in for Ruth and carry her out; her body's soft but heavy. I almost drop her by the car. I'm pouring with sweat.

"It'll be all right, honey sweetheart, it'll be fine." I kiss her head and gently place her in the trunk.

I'm driving, wondering when she'll wake, telling myself I didn't hit her that hard, it was a tap. A little tap. Once we reach the highway we'll be better, I'll pull over, lift her into the back, we'll drive, go to a motel. God I love her. . . . I'm seeing her body sprawled out now on a double bed, loose, letting me kiss into her navel. I'm so involved with her navel I fail to notice the Toyota 4 x 4. They wave, I wave, hoh, hoh, mirror action. Robbie, Tim,

Yvonne. I'll do what they do. They don't seem real to me—chatty holograms that have to be dealt with. I wipe my face with the skirt.

"Hello! Hi there."

Robbie's driving, he shouts at me, "Hi, how's she running?"

"What?"

"The car."

"Ohh, good."

"Good."

"Have you seen Ruth?" I initiate.

Tim looks at me and whispers. Robbie looks, and whispers back.

"Arh, no" says Robbie. "Where is she?"

Cough, "I was hoping you might know. So she's not up at the homestead?"

"No, she's not." Tim's mouth is decidedly stiff, he lights a cigarette.

"So what the fuck happened—has she taken off?"

My throat's tickling so much I can't control it and start to cough badly. *Hack, hack.* Out of the corner of my eye, I notice necks, some of them moving. More necks.

It's those weird staccato birds, the emus.

"WELL?!" yells Tim. "Has she taken OFF?!"

"That's it." *Hack, hack.* "She's gone and we'd better get after her. I'm going over to check the bar." I get into gear and there's fucking birds blocking, so I can't drive off. Yvonne steps out from Robbie's car and is walking through them. An emu lunges at her, she screams at it, swinging out with her handbag. "I'm coming with yoouu!"

Shit, *why? "*Yvonne! It's not necessary."

She opens the passenger door.

I repeat, "It's not necessary." She's immune, her eyes bat in rapid flutter.

"I'm coming, Robbie asked me to. He thinks she may need a woman. You're not a woman, you don't understand all the physical torments we have to go through."

She settles in and fastens her seat belt, her face open, unconcerned, free. I try to assume the same carefree attitude.

"So, when did this happen?"

"An hour, hour and a half ago."

"Oh dear."

Robbie honks the horn, the emus scatter. He parks up nearer to us. SHIT.

"Yes?"

"Um, when did she . . . leave, precisely?"

(Rewind.) "About an hour, hour and a half ago."

"How come?"

"I was napping."

"So it could have been longer?" I shrug my shoulders. Tim clicks his tongue, *"You,"* aggressively implied, not said.

He tosses a half-smoked cigarette out the window, the end burns fiercely red. I want one.

"Could I have a cigarette, please?"

"Thought you didn't smoke. . . ."

"I don't." He passes one. I say: "You better go back and check the hut, see if she's come back."

"Okay," Robbie leans out and lights me, immediately I feel ill. Light-headed manic, got to get away. I know Tim wants to berate me further, but can't articulate the full litany of my wrongdoing. Mirror, mirror, what does he see? A sweaty, tense face, smudged eyeliner, *lipstick*. I wave them on, grinding out in third, cigarette tasting awful, everything fairly tarnished. I offer the cigarette to Yvonne—she doesn't want it either, she wants to talk.

"I hope Ruth's been behaving herself. Young women can be such big teasers, I should know, hee, hee." She pats my thigh gingerly, exploring, bare flesh running into skirt, to—"ARH!" Her eyes dart 'round. Instant confusion.

"Oh golly, that looks a little like my top."

"Well it is."

Another high pitched, "ARH!" I ignore her, not sure of the direction, the car bumps over rocks.

"Hmmm . . . Actually, I feel sorry for Ruth, because I've been thinking about it and I don't think there is anything out there, just a BIG blank nothing." Her face is unusually flushed.

Bang, bang. There's a soft thumping from the trunk. *Bang.* I turn on the radio.

"Oh yes, I love music, mood music, hmmm. What was I saying . . . oh, yes, nothing! If you sit and think about it, it can swallow you up. I've seen it. I saw it with

Robbie when he lost his job. Brooding in front of the videos, nonstop videos. One day I just said to him, 'Robbie! Robbie, you've got to choose, you've got to be happy, beee . . .'"

"What?"

Yvonne's silent. "Yvonne, what?" Her stillness freaks me out. She's listening, she can hear Ruth banging in the trunk. I touch her leg, she shrieks, "STOP IT! STOP THE CAR! Oh God! Oh my GOD!! I know where she is, the little idiot! That is so dangerous. RUUUTH!"

We slide to a halt in speeding numbness. Fuck, why didn't I think of the heat! Jesus. Sudden lucid fear, icy hands pulling at the trunk release. *Bang, Baaang!* Yvonne squawking in my ear.

"Ruth, Ruth, it's Yvonne, I don't care who you believe in, you've gone too far. You could have killed yourself, you little idiot!!"

My legs wobble to the trunk, "Is she all right? Is she all right?"

She doesn't look it. She's covered in red dust, with a big trickle of blood running down her nose. Yvonne is yelping, helping her out. "Arrh hm, Arrh hm." She stands unsteadily, gulping air.

I try to say: "It's all right Ruth," like I had nothing to do with it. Comes out a whisper, hardly audible.

Yvonne echoes me. "Yes, it's all right, we are helping you."

I put my hand out, Ruth shrinks from me; "No!"

manoeuvres herself behind Yvonne, clutching at her clothes. Yvonne hugs her. "It's okay Ruthie, don't be scared, don't be frightened."

She seems ill, not listening. Peels herself physically from Yvonne, shuffles backwards. I try to catch her but I'm limping without shoes. I get in the car and start to drive, Yvonne dithers in between us. "Wait, Wait!" she shouts.

"I can't, I have to go."

Ruth stumbles on in front of me, it's rocky, crumbly earth. She slips and slides, I'm almost on her.

"I love you, I love you, I love you. . . . Please get back in the car."

She turns to me, shakes her head, and laughs, disembodied, loud.

"All right! All right! I care about you then! We'll go to India, I'm truly sorry."

I pull the car up, cut her off. She goes rigid, her face furious, wordless, she veers up a small hillside strewn with boulders. Impossible to follow, so I jump out, don't stop the car, just let it run off . . . putt, putt, something for Yvonne to follow. It's a steep climb, we're scrambling up along the shady side towards a plateaued peak. She's kicking rocks down at me as she goes. The tension inside me's imploding, my stomach feels fucked up, piercing me in spasms. I'm hauling up through dust and rubble, frantically pulling up my body, vomiting, wiping it away. I can get her back, I know I can, it's my talent, it's my job.

This is all part of it, she's got to see I'll walk on glass for her.

"Oh God, Ruth, come on stop, what can I do? RUTH, RUTH!! Look, Ruth, see . . . I lick the earth, see, I'll eat dirt for you, just forgive me. PLEASE ! You want Baba? We'll go to Baba. I'll take you, he'll help us."

She's staring down at me from the peak. Her head haloed by the sun, glowing with light, her face is dark.

"PJ, your knees are bleeding."

I kind of laugh, and look at them, they are pretty bloody, especially the right. "Ruth are you going to help? You going to help me Ruth?"

I look up to study the effect, but she's gone.

19

I can see two figures, one static, one moving. And one empty Falcon, coasting down the valley in the opposite direction, bob, bob, bob, blaring inarticulate jumble from the stereo. I watch to see what the figures are doing, especially him, he is motionless and seems to be watching Yvonne, who jogs along in her heels, arm pointing in the car's direction. It's so hot they haze into molten blobs of colour. He walks towards her, she runs backwards, bending down for something . . . Rocks? Yes, rocks, she hugs them to her chest. He moves, hops towards her, she tosses her rocks at his feet, there's no resistance from him, he stops and hangs his head. She runs off up the valley.

My head's aching, I have no water, the paperbacks slow me down. I tremble uncontrollably, what if I'd died in the boot? In that stifling tomb. Fuck, it was awful, the whole thought seems worse than ever now I'm saved. When I woke I thought I was buried. I was beside myself with panic, shoving my hands out, frantically feeling into every hole. Searching everywhere for openings and there weren't any. Then I knew I was in a boot, being tossed, my head bumping against the bump he'd already given me. I thought he loved me and wouldn't want to hurt me. If Yvonne hadn't been there he might have punched me out. He didn't look as if he'd punch me out, he looked terrified. The whole incident makes me want to cry, I feel my lips collapsing at the thought, tears spurt out of me. Why didn't I take the car when it was sitting there, why didn't I? I can't see why and I can't see why he knocked me out.

I feel the bump on my head. It's sore below the crown, there's a podgy swelling, painfully nice to touch. It's his fault, he told me to push him, to do my worst. I didn't even do my worst. I don't know what that worst would be. I don't really have violent thoughts. Other people have them for me. Mum says I could drive a saint to slaughter but I don't see it. Maybe that's it, my no slaughter makes them want to do the slaughter for me, that's the theory. Though I'm not sure how it works. I don't want to think of it. I suppose I could have carried on bitching at him, but that's just words. I made him love me, that was my worst; my worst was I didn't love him.

What I couldn't stand was being stuck inside my mind. Endless bloody power games, going on and on and nowhere. Crazy rages about him . . . I felt like the insides of my head were being torn and punched apart and every time they'd settle there'd be another punch and another fucked-up argument to fix. Bang.

My head is boiling, I take my pants off and put them on my head . . . this is my punishment for bonking him, stuck in the desert in a terrible outfit. Exposed. At least out here everything can be seen. Blue grass, red splotches on the hills. Boulders, salt grass, more boulders on top of hillocks. Blue grass, boulders, red earth, yellow earth, uninterrupted sun and sky.

God! I'm just so mad. Why did I have to tell him all those things about myself. Ooh, Yuck, FUCK. I hate it that he knows—all my needy internal cravings with bloody Baba, to have him love me, to have myself loved and appreciated by somebody. Yah, I hate it. It makes me want to throw myself on the ground and drum my heels in rage.

The sun is burning, sizzling its way into my flesh. I don't even care that I'm burning, it's a relief. My head still aches from the pressure. I walk about a kilometre, I can see little hillocks and boulders that seemed close when I first looked at them, but in reality are much further away. At the third boulder, I start to think of him again.

I bet he does this job to get love, to have people fawn around and tell him how insightful he is. What happened to me probably always happens: kiss, kiss, "I'm sorry, thank you for showing me the way." Except they don't fuck him. I hope I taught that disgusting old sex scrotum a lesson. Probably couldn't believe his luck, probably gave him what he wanted. God. That is a problem. He's so bloody selfish anyway—we're both so bloody selfish, I want my way and he wants his. All that stuff about there being only three people in the world who could ever truly love me . . .

Then. I'm looking up at the deep blue sky with its cut-out clouds sitting there perfectly shaped and still, when it hits upon me, as a bolt from heavens that . . . that old disgusting sex manic slob IS the only person who has ever truly loved me!!!

AHHHHHH! God! What a horrible realisation. Ahhhhh. It sickens me.

Why?

Yes why?

It just does.

What does it matter.

Walk, walk, I didn't expect it.

And you did love him, or let yourself be loved by him. Yes, yes, yesss. I start to laugh. He did love you, you let him love you, you did, you didn't, you did. Oh Blah, Blah, Blah, BLAH!

There's a trillion, million, cattle scratches on the earth, hoofprint scars. I stop to look at them, well, I look at a whirly whirly, coming up out the corner of my eye and distracting me. They're all over the place, mini pink tornadoes, invisible unless they suck up sand. Three cockatoos fly overhead, just zoom through, don't even notice me. I look at the variegated cattle lines, one of these will take me into the hills. I choose the one with the most impressions, walk, walk, walk, putting one foot in front of the other. Then the hoofprints run out.

Up ahead there's a mound I'm going to aim for. It has a red swirl on top. The swirl is in fact a patch of sand and in front of the mound there's another ridge, which I couldn't see before. I sit down, dry-mouthed, in a lovely golden haze, slightly cooler, shadows growing out 'round hills. Two wild emus—they go in pairs, Puss says they always do—munching at the grass. Must re-tie, re-bandage, the raggedy daggy old feet. Stare down at my hands: "Do it!" I say, they don't move, they don't look like mine. They look like moulds you pour plaster of Paris into. I wonder if they could just crawl off without me or if I could just get up and leave my body behind, turn 'round, see where I was and come back down again.

According to Baba, that's what we do, inhabit bodies and sit around in railway stations, on a platform waiting for a train. Spend our time on this earth like passengers ready to move on, nobody will meet again. The train will leave and will never come back to the same station. Some people sit around and picnic, others manage to set up a few stores, some dash about entertaining, and one or two read the destination.

If my body really is a stocking, and incidental, then I want to know what I borrowed it for. And if I can stand behind that body and observe it, it could mean there is also something standing behind my substance self with a purpose. If I could get to that, *that thing,* I might know what the purpose was. It was clear to me that the body was the functional me, the volatile me—but the substance me I couldn't get to.

My borrowed body vibrates. I look down. The sand shudders around my foot, it stops and shudders again. I get up and walk down the mound and across to the next hill, where the shudderings increase. At the top of the hill I see fence posts half buried in the sand. I follow the fence posts down, watching the sand shaking on the tops. I look up and see the red side of a truck whooshing past.

20

Every inch of my aching self wants to confess to Ruth.
Confession, absolution, blessing. (To be blessed by her, that
would be something.) I never appreciated the point
of all that ritual when I was growing up, but now I can
see the attraction: the surrender of self to the judgment of the wise. Forgiveness. Forgive me Lord, for I'm
wearing a virtual bikini, thanks to the shrunken state of this
girlie, belly-piercing top, plus I've had to rip up the skirt to
wrap around my shoeless feet. The backs of my arms and
neck are burning, my head, calves and face are burning—all
thanks to the brotherly cavalry riding to the rescue.

The buzzing in my head has stopped, and the shuf-
fling of my feet sounds deafening in this noise vacuum of
a landscape. Feet and flies become the next overriding
preoccupation, the flies get flicked, the feet are pierced
by every other yard of sharply felt earth. I have to find
her. All I want to do is to kiss and make up. Explain it
was never my intention to injure her, deflate her, enter
her little head games, none of that. All I initially wanted
was to introduce a level of personal vigilance and well,
frankly, fuck her, though I didn't see that coming.
Anyway, it's not just a fuck. It's an in-love situation
where no one else will do.

Ruth, this is what I must confess: I don't need black
rooms—you are my fantasy—though if you ever wanted

one I'd accommodate and decorate. I'd like to think there is nothing we couldn't do together. You could express yourself however you wanted and not be spied upon. I don't like to be spied on either, though I suspect I'd mind less than you. Maybe not, maybe superficially I feel less self-conscious, my presentation more reasoned. The truth is I've let myself go.

Right now I'm in an inexorable mess, unprotected from the sun, no water, flies buzzing 'round my bloodied knees. I rub dirt into them hoping it'll stop the bleeding. Then walk and work on my apology.

Oh Ruth, I apologise. That's the basic title.

Ruth, there's nothing forgivable in my actions, I love you, I panicked, I'm a fool. I felt if you went that would be the end. You're young (as you keep reminding me), too young to know how rare certain chemistries are. I had to do it, maybe you'll thank me some day, when we're cosied up together.

Apology Number Two.

Sweetheart, I lost my head over you and hit yours. No. But truly sweetheart, I'm sorry. This is no excuse but not many women are as stubborn as you, as totally unavailable once you decide to wall off. And I do admire your strength. It's infuriating but I admire it.

Three.

We live in the Kali-yuga age, the iron age of quarrel

and materialism—maybe that's why we quarrel, we're not in control, we're not telepathic. Hindu scriptures declare that an earth such as ours is dissolved for one of two reasons: the inhabitants as a whole become either completely good or completely evil. The world mind thus generates a power that releases the captive atoms held together as an earth. We two, or too—I was going to say, "atoms"—but this is just a crude attempt to capture Indian interests. "Don't make me vomit," I can hear you say it.

Four.

Ruth, I'm sorry. What can I do to reassure you? It was a moment of madness, I didn't want to lose you or my professional grip, I lost both. I am not a violent man. Believe me. I was possessed, frightened. Please try and view events in the light of me wishing you well. Truly, I believe in you.

P.S. I guess you have the power to hurt me, I don't have many defences against that.

To be cruel there's the distinct possibility she doesn't dig me, that maybe it was just a game for her. My mind flashes back to that—"I, I, I tricked you"—hand thumping against her chest in the bedroom. But that was before, at the height of her rage and the beginning of our—love affair?

Or it could be I'm not reading it right, because for some inexplicable reason I expect those I'm infatuated with to be infatuated with me. I can accept some crushes are not reciprocal, though I've never been particularly curious to discover wherein I am less than attractive. I tend to rationalise rejections, as so and so's "fear" or "unavailability." Maybe she was punishing me, testing my faith in her. Ruth: I could and can see myself packing up and moving right on in, that's the feeling. She's bold, passionate, not obsessed with money, a seeker like myself. Most people are riddled with fears, she has hers, not about the outside world, about herself. Oh hell. Obviously I wanted some mad last passionate fling. Forget it. You hit her, you knocked her down, she hates your guts. . . .

RUUTH, RROOUTH! ROOUTH! RRooUth!

I lie, hoarse from screeching out her name . . . and doze. Flies buzz in my face so the skirt reconstitutes as a face shader. I wake up with a start, no idea how much time has passed, sun still hot and high, and I'm shaking with fear: Ruth is not out there lying prettily arranged on a boulder, she's suffering a major breakdown, wandering in heat and unfamiliar landscape, jabbering off phoney guru nonsense: "Actually only the body can be slain, actually your material world and mundane reasoning are a veil before God. Actually you are not your body.

Actually, actually, actually . . ." It's so possible I jump up—what have I done? I've failed. Totally failed to contain the client, left the containment area—and of course fucking the client, doesn't matter that she's damn well throwing herself at you. You don't take it up, because they don't want you! They just don't want themselves. Basics. Still, I don't regret it though, I regret the dishonesty. I should have come clean. It's not exactly going to be our little secret anymore. I should have confronted the situation, spoken to Tim.

Me: "Excuse me, but I've had sex with your sister."

Tim : "You what?!!"

Me: "Yees, she begged me to. She asked me to have sex with her, couldn't help it (pathetic). I love your sister and I'm afraid I slept with her (hero)."

Tim: "What about the—excuse me—deprogramming?"

Me: "It shouldn't affect it."

Tim: "Crap!"

Me: "It shouldn't affect it unduly."

Tim and Robbie beat me to a pulp, egged on by an indignant Yvonne.

I tie the skirt back round my foot and hop step in what I hope to be an easterly direction. There's very little cover so logic dictates she'll be found, I'll be found. I've got to speak with her before the others, that's the main objective, try to agree on some last-minute boundaries. Why? Yes why? You haven't controlled her—*I've given her my personal best*. Yes, and if she's going to make shit with it she's going to make shit with it: "What is crooked cannot be made straight, and what is lacking cannot be numbered."

Errup, errup, errup, I walk through pale yellow grass, two carrion crows ahead, their dense black plumage stands out from the dried pink dust. I'm sure I've seen the tatty one at the hut. His eye has no expression, dead. Shark rolling in a feeding frenzy. He watches, he'd watch anything the same, everything's the same. He hops along beside me, stops when I stop. I shout, panicky, thinking he's waiting for me to die. I lose my footing, tumbling down into a riverbed, an abandoned road winding through thick clusters of skeletal trees. I feel shocked, unwell. I shut my eyes and see the cell phone sitting in the hut, right beside the sewing kit she fingered. Why didn't I give it to her?

RUUUOOOTH!!

She's right—I am a salivating old slob who wants to sleep with her. The way she pulls herself up and looks with that enigmatic smile, not quite telling, firmly present. I love the earnest drive as well, when she's so . . . so kind of gooey naked (can't think about naked). I just love her, that's all, despite all the attacking resistance, all the acts of—shit.

"Ruth?"

"Yes?"

"I was talking about you . . ."

"Yes?"

"Saying very attractive, affectionate things."

"Don't make me mad about this will you?"

"I'm not mad."

"No, I know you're not."

"Let me kiss your feet."

"Look, I don't want you to."

"Just your feet."

"All right. You can kiss them, my feet are very sore."

21

The joke is I'm on the highway and there haven't been any trucks or cars, none since that red truck. The road represented such bliss to me, I ran down into it expecting immediate rescue, so now my legs feel weak. I have to sit down, mistake. I look into the tarmac, which shines and oozes and mesmerises me. Masses of swirling, sizzling heat ripples, my head fights an overwhelming need to snooze.

Spooky wake-up—as though someone or something was watching over me. The road is clear, there's absolutely nothing, no living thing in sight. I tell myself not to con-jure him, it'll be twice as bloody painful if I do, my head hurts with the effort to stop this giving over of myself, to try and focus. To figure out what direction's going where. I wouldn't know east from west, the sun sets in the west, the sun is a fiery egg. I feel up on my head, no pants. Shit, I find myself stumbling along the road on a pants hunt, not sure if I was wearing them when I slept. Christ, I can't take care of anything, even a pair of pants is beyond me. I'm so anxious to find them, I rush excit-edly to plastic bags and wonder if I can wear them tied together in a napkin.

The plastic disintegrates into stretchy chewing gum under pressure, this makes me feel like fucking death, a toilet nightmare without walls. I don't even know how much is visible, I press the T-towel to see whether my pubes poke through, great! I can't even tell. I'm twisting round in circles with this stupid inspection lark—nothing's even coming. I hardly dare look I feel so bloody nervous. Two cars come, a family, a woman driver wearing shades with kids, she waves, I wave, she drives right on past me waving. I sort of go, blink! and can't quite believe she . . . did. The second car comes, a Volvo, I step into the road, smile, wave, smile—the Volvo slows. A man. He drives carefully up towards me, looks, stops, looks. Short browny hair, Raybans, moustache. I rush out after him wheezing, "HELP Me! HELP, Help me. . . ." The paperbacks scuff and hurt my toes. He screeches off, chunks of paper blow into the road. I must look weird, I do, I am weird. No one is going to pick me up.

My mind is getting skittish, I can't decide what side of the road I should be on and want to invest the cars with meaning. Lovely stopping cars, hateful indifference. I stick to the verge, looking meek, cars still reject me—a truck, a car. I try to look more sympathetic, you have to present a certain way, semidepressed, not desperate. I meekly wave at a distant car. It toots and slows, flashing its lights. God . . . it's Dad, happily smiling his head off. Chiselled white-yellow mannequin teeth, he veers up alongside me, coasting forward. I feel otherworldly, not quite there. Afraid. Bill Bill's sitting beside him, madly yelling, "Ruth! Ruth!"

Dad joins in, "Oh Ruthie . . . Christ! You're burnt. Get in! Get in!"

I don't . . . don't want to. Say, "I need water."

"Of course you do darls, hop in."

His voice is unnaturally high, he hangs the water bottle out the window. "Come on dear, get in, get in."

I don't. "Water," I say. All I really see is the water bottle. Dad gets out, he's bare-chested. There's tension between us. Bill Bill's nervous, very giggly, ha, ha, ha, we've never been enemies before. We tell Sinatra jokes, every cunt wants to sing my way. "*Come on Ruthie*, drink, take it in sups." His hand rests on the bottom of the bottle, he raises it to my lips.

"Small sups." They're both scrutinising me, nudging hips. "I," Ruth, have vanished, they're looking at an object: "Baby," who's wearing rubbish, walking on the highway, an aimless crybaby. I am, I am an aimless baby. I'm watching, waiting for them to do things to me. Dad sidles up to me, "Come on, we can't stand here all day." He reaches for the bottle, I snatch it back.

"Dad, he knocked me out."

"Did he? Well that's very bad. Where is he?"

"Dad, you're not listening to me."

"Yes we are, we are listening, aren't we, Bill Bill?"

"Yes," says Bill Bill. "We are listening, Ruth, we've come out here to help you."

Whack! The bottle's smacked away. It bounces high off the gravel into the road. I limp off after it, hobbling up the bank.

"LEFT!! Bill, go left!"

They split apart, coming at me from either side. "Get her legs, get her legs."

I sit, head down, scrunched in a ball.

"Dad, I'm not going to the police."

"Good on you, darling, you've always been a believer. Bill thinks you're on to something, don't you Bill Bill?"

"Yes, we do."

"Dad, he knocked me out."

"Yes, I heard that . . . but you said you'd stay."

I haven't the strength, I give up, I don't care anymore, I really don't. "Okay then. Run me over."

"What?"

"Just take the car and run me down."

I bury my head and hear them muttering near me, I hear a cigarette lighter, a passing vehicle, and brakes. Door, footsteps, gravel.

Dad yells, "Psychiatric, she's got problems upstairs—we've got to get her to the hospital."

An enormous hand spans the width of my head, fingers pulling at my temples. It's joined to the hugest arm and flattest, squarest head I've ever seen. We look at each other. I can sense he feels uncertain. We stand there blinking in the sun, our eyes are talking. His are teenie weenie gray, mine speak rapidly: "You know I'm not mad, don't you? I'm frightened, that's all."

He says, "My brother's schizophrenic."

I can't think what to say, so I say, "Does he wear books?"

He laughs and asks me if they work?

I say, "Not very well. They moult."

He laughs again, "Are you all right?"

I say, "No, not really. I feel unwell."

Their hands grope out and try to lift me. My diaphragm flexes uncontrollably, makes dry, involuntary gagging sounds. Coughing and stooping, I dry retch into the ground. I spy a stone and pick it up, my fingers closing over sharp, hard, edges. I focus on a white pickup truck. It's slowing, creep, creep, into my stone arm, my arm goes stiff with anticipation.

Dad and Bill Bill step into the road.

The ute brakes and swerves towards them.

Dad and Bill Bill go to the cab, Bill Bill runs back and forth with blankets.

Tim and Robbie get out, light cigarettes.

Yvonne leans over the back tray.

Robbie shouts at Dad.

Bill Bill points to me.

The stone is sticky when Timmy hugs me, he takes me to view PJ, lying on the back of the tray. He's bleeding, broken down, and hideous. I can't bear it. Dad kicks out at Robbie, tears run down my face. Robbie and Dad punch each other. I scream at them, I don't want him to die.

The stone is still in my hand when we arrive at the motel (Carol's strategy for recovery). Mum bathes it in warm water, stupid really; I have to have it back, even stupider. Mum calls a doctor.

I tell the doctor about the stone. She gets Valium. She's not that old or tall. Short, fat, and blonde with lots of freckles on podgy arms, we talk alone. She wants to know if I was raped. I shake my head.

"Consensual sex?"

I nod.

"Were you using contraceptives?"

I shake my head.

"Do you want the morning-after pill?"

I nod.

She tells me I'll have to apply ointment to the sunburn, she wants me to apply it for a week. I'm not to use perfumes, makeup, perfumed shampoos or soaps, or any other lotions with scents or strong ingredients.

There's a silence while she writes up the prescription.

"Uh-huh." I cough and point to the door.

"Are they listening?"

She looks up. "Who?"

I feel dumb and look into my hands . . . I can hear her breathing. After an agonising minute she twists herself off the bed and pokes her nose around the door.

"Nope." She sits back down again. "What is it you want to tell me?"

"Well you know the American man."

"The one you slept with?"

"Yes." God. Said completely unabashed, my face flushes I don't know why, they all know, maybe that's it—*they do all know.* I sort of do and don't care. Pressing the bed with my stone.

"I want to know where he is."

Her eyes are on me, "Hmm."

"I just wanted to know how he is. Is he in hospital?"

"Yes." She looks long and hard at me, her eyes boring in, I smile long and hard back, we look at my stone pounding the sheet. . . . it's satisfying to the point of giggling. I give it to her.

She says, "Thank you." She probably doesn't even want it, which sets me off giggling again at the thought of her having to take it home.

She says, "Well done."

Hmmm, that's it. I hold on for seconds, proud nodding, then burst into shameless hysterics.

I wake to an oxygen mask in a square dark room, with lights from another low-rise building beaming in. Dull pulse, my right leg's throbbing. A tube is taped to a mass of cotton wool and plaster, it takes a moment to register this hand as mine. Freak out. I'm not sure I want to see the damage. Even the slightest movement sends interesting stabs of pain into all my extremities. Two observations dominate: I'm alive and I'm alone.

The last thing I remember was Ruth dancing in a sari, twenty Ruths, all multiplying and birthing out of this one gargantuan statue of her. They landed and broke up in little wriggles of mercury. Still dancing. They'd go all the way to the left, wobble. And traverse all the way to the right. Ethereal karaoke, very beautiful, she did this stamping thing with her foot. Bali Hai, my little darling, come to me, come to me.

There is a drinks tray conveniently pushed as far away from me as possible. I'm obviously in a hospital, double dose of the helpless, no buzzer to locate, no fucking one around, not even Carol. Especially Carol . . . depends what's been said of course, not that she's so broad-minded. She's not. If Yvonne's been coughing up all the soggy detail, she might not be understanding. In fact, forget it, this is quarantine. At least I won't have to listen to it all. Chewed out, over again.

"And then he said he wanted to share her underwear and her makeup, and make love to her as another woman."

"Oh no [cascades of no-ness], he didn't, did he?"

"He did! He did! He said. Well, apparently, he felt closer to her that way"

"I think it's disgusting!"

Disgusting! Revelations further extended by Robbie's porn repertoire. She was forced to *blank, blank* (fill in the gaps) until her *blank* went numb. And then the— God! . . . I'll mail a check.

Devil dick. I breathe in the humiliation, normal air's too good for me.

They must have found her. She couldn't have been far from me. I look for a clock, I thought all hospitals had clocks. This is not me. I'm almost slightly impressed by the not knowing of times and dates. It's definitely foreign, a virus, a condition I'd always feared; being less or discovered as less. Less brainy, less organized, less coherent—less *hot shot*. I don't, for example know what day it is—the twenty-third, or the fourth? Which is funny until you actually don't know what day it is . . .

Ruth, I love you, an' I'm gonna to get to that drinks tray, I'm going to cruise in on neutral and take that water, no food. Purify.

6:00 a.m. on the twenty-fourth, I've ruined Christmas.
Mum drives me to the hospital. She loathes Christmas, I
haven't ruined Christmas, I've cheered her up: big distraction, very happy. She keeps reaching over and squeezing my
hand: "Are you alright darling?" squeeze, pulverise. "Haah,
I'm so, so, sorry darling," and, "How are you now?" All of
which secretly pleases me.

When we pull up at the hospital, I'm awkward, we sit
there, silent. Then Mum says, "We-elll."

I say, "What? What is it you want to say?"

"Well," she says and strokes my forehead, "you don't
have to do this, you know"—fingers tucking in a strand
of hair—"if you want to, we can just turn around and
drive straight back."

I go in alone, pink galahs squawking from a tree. Inside
it's cool, gray and shiny, my palms sweat. I walk in without a skin, as if everyone can see through me, and view
the sexual goings-on. Pushing into the toilet I wash my
hands, drink, and pee. I don't know what I've come to
do, all I know is I have to sort of finish with him. The
main anxiety is the way I do this, uncomplicated is how I
wish it, but I'm not sure I can . . . can be like this. Room
113, a hundred and thirteen, big arrow left. Crinkle ceil-

ings with light skid-marked floors, strip lighting, children's drawings, and turquoise curtains. The point is I
don't think I could have not seen him, that's the point—
Mum knew, she was good about it.

His room's at the end of a long corridor, opposite a
large sunny window. There's a Do Not Disturb sign on
the door. My hand reaches out and clicks . . . midturn, I
stop, twist, and close it again. I drift around in front of
the window, watching parrots hop about on the lawn, the
grass has lots of dry patches, tracks worn bare through to
the car park. A couple of nurses chatter under a tree,
they're laughing and drinking from bright white plastic
disposable cups. The nurse in the pale blue cardigan
takes her shoes off, rubs her foot against the trunk. The
other nurse has got a bag of Poppers. She opens them,
spilling some out on the lawn. The parrots go crazy. . . .
That is normal life, I'm thinking.

Maybe it's the idea of going back into a confined space
with him: his room and the room being *his*. God, this is
stupid, really shitty, having monster hallucinations of
him. It didn't happen in the moments face to face, I
could see who he was. Only when we separated would he
blow up on me. I'd create him bigger than he was—
EVIL. When we sat down again I'd see him as ordinary,
and be disappointed in the amount of puff I'd puffed
into him. I found him disappointing in the flesh and

craved this other weird, exciting, powerful person and wondered if he had some other self he'd carefully packed into the wardrobe.

My fear is, if I go into that room and he says just one wrong thing, I might go mad and completely lose it. Logically, I can't imagine what that one thing could possibly be.

What am I going to say anyway? That I had a few demons and doubts? Like lots. Like: you're in it for the money, you're a fucked-up individual who wears shitty clothes, a charlatan and I don't have to take fake interpretations from you. I don't have to take them because you're nothing and there's nothing wrong with me. You're not good enough. You can't get beyond the hate of your guru. Anything revealing I told you about myself, you used against me. Used it to give yourself power over me. Everyone wants power. Only the weak are weak and the strong forbear, the strong rule. I'm judgmental because the world judges and that's the standard. I could say that.

And he'd say, "Ruth, you have a very nice bod . . ."

No, he'd say, "Ahh. Could you please read your *forehead!*"

I turn the handle. The room is darkened and so quietly silent I know he's asleep. In my head he was pretending sleep; all the better to grab me. But it's crap. His eyelids, lips, and scalp are blistered and swollen, every bit of him is bandaged, smothered in cream. His head seems twice its normal size and there are stitches on his forehead above the brow. I want to touch him but am afraid. I'm frightened in general he looks so sick and, in a funny way, like Frankenstein's monster. I go over to the basin, look at my own puffed-up face in the mirror and don't know what to do. Eventually, I find a scrap of paper and write:

I liked it. Not all of it. Love Ruth.

Dear P J,

So far I've seen six guru / holy men and one holy
woman. All the men said I was wasting my time,
they'd heard Australia was a wonderful country and
very rich, more or less why give up sense for chaos. The
woman said, You do not need to marry, you need to
know God is everything. I told her I still didn't get the
purpose of this particular "I" I now inhabit. She
laughed. I still think it's a valid question. Mum and me
bumble on. I did wonder if irritations with her were
actually mine, but dismissed this. She could still be irritating, takes forever to get ready, chats unnecessarily
to stoned people, and looks too long at "things," ruins
for example. Gets on very well with <u>Holies</u>.

One man said many holy men were jealous of one
another and hadn't renounced a thing. He said sannyasins were parasites unable to face worldly responsi-
bilities and when I asked him about self realisation he
said he was too busy helping the poor. Hint, hint, he
had one lazy eye, the good one doing twice the penetrating, we worked with his charity for a week—the old
Cyclops guilt trip. He took us to his school where children were playing with rubbish, toys made from old
tin cans and string. One girl showed me her cat, a
lump of rubber tyre she'd woven wool into, blubber,

blubber. Next address, Animal Suffering in Jaipur-
Durgapur, Rajasthan, Mum's idea. Not sure what I'll
be doing, Mum thinks pooh removal.

Ohhh yes, I've got a boyfriend, he's a little jealous of
you and I don't blame him. I don't know why I love you
but I do—from afar. What happened out there?
Something did happen, didn't it?

Love
Ruth

Dear Celestial Searcher,

Thank you for your letter and news. What about this. Carol and I are the proud parents of twins! We invite you to our wedding—June 22nd. She's forgiven me, patched me up, chewed me out, nursed me (note role reversal.) Not a swift transition, let me tell you. Personally, very challenging . . . and you know how I appreciate that. I'm a novelist now, on to my second book, a tale set in the Aussie outback, based on this detective's investigation into the disappearance of a beautiful young woman. Titled: My Avenging Angel. Yes? In it, I pose this question: "What did she want?" Well?

Could you really love me? I'm amazed even if it is from far, far, away—I wear it like a blessing. About the "something," yes, didn't you notice it just about killed me!

Yours anytime (don't tell Carol)

Waters

Dear Waters,

Was corrected by "hippie" in Sarnath: Buddhism is a philosophy, not a religion. This said very loud at Dharmarajiki stupa site of Buddha's first sermon. Shame. Had a blissful yoga camp in Rishikesh, wonderful teacher, he said to sow the seeds of love into the situation rather than waiting for a change in fucked world order. We are now in Jaipur. Mum is in her element, picking lice and healing wounds—I'm cleaning cages.

About your question—What does she want?—She wants to know things but doesn't always want to accept them. Reeeaaally accept them. She wants to say crap, that the question is impossible. Right now she wants something sweet to eat.

OM.

R.

Ruth wandered in the land.

'Oh it is a wilderness.'

She came upon rotting bones

And finally a little bush

Which upon her gaze

Burst into flames.

Ruth remembered Margaret Hart from her school days,

The girl who had heard the words of God.

Watching the burning Bush, Ruth felt sure God existed.

This was his language and she knew by day's end she would know its meaning.

She turned and walked, the sun upon her back, her shadow falling across the earth. She looked upon her shadow and saw it was a large keyhole, so she turned, as if she herself were the key. And walked sun on face towards the big fiery orb. Her shadow falling dark and long behind her. In this way she walked towards the setting sun.

BIBLIOGRAPHY

Robert Jay Lifton. *Thought Reform and the Psychology of Totalism (A Study of "Brainwashing" in China)*. Pelican Books, 1967. First published in the U.S.A. 1961.

Steve Hassan. *Combating Cult Mind Control*. Park Street Press, Rochester, Vermont, 1990.

Tal Brooke. *Lord of the Air (Tales of a Modern Antichrist)*. Harvest House Publishers, Eugene, Oregon, 1990.

Paramahansa Yoganada. *Autobiography of a Yogi (A Major Classic of Indian Spirituality)*. Rider, Imprint of Ebury Press, Random House, 1996. First published in 1946.

Larry D. Shinn. *The Dark Lord (Cult Images and the Hare Krishnas In America)*. The Westminster Press, Philadelphia, 1987.

Irina Tweedie. *The Chasm of Fire (A Woman's Experience of Liberation Through the Teachings of a Sufi Master)*. Element Classics Edition, Great Britain, 1993.

William Shaw. *Spying in Guru Land (Inside Britain's Cults)*. Fourth Estate, London, 1995.

Brian Lane. *Killer Cults (Murderous Messiahs and their Fanatical Followers)*. Headline Book Publishing, 1997.

Bhagavad Gita. *The Song of God, Translated by Swami Prabhavananda and Christopher Isherwood*. J. M. Dent & Sons LTD, 1976. First published in 1947.